Outer

Space

Casino

D1607820

Tom Norton

DEDICATION

To those who would rather write a book than read one.

CONTENTS

CONTENTS

FOREWORD

This is a story that takes place around the year 2270. Now it is just conjecture what the Earth, Mars and the Moon will be like at that time, but for the purpose of this story, the backdrop is one of many possible scenarios for the future, but possibly not far off.

In this story's scenario that is not described in detail, the Earth itself has endured coastal flooding covering some of the coastal areas and there is mention of a contaminated area due to most likely a nuclear reactor accident. This has little to do with the story itself, but the Earth's society and infrastructure at the time does.

Today we travel through towns and cities that have been there for a hundred or two hundred years and portions of the towns or cities look just like they did a hundred or two hundred years earlier. People are still living in these houses and the business buildings are still functioning. This being the case, it is not hard to imagine in the year 2270 there are buildings, businesses and housing that remain the same and the people there are little different than they were when the buildings were new. Like we now see around us, advanced technology and infrastructure flourish in some areas of the society and not in others.

The theme of this story pertains to early twentieth century mobs, gangs and hoodlums, the resulting movies made about them and the influence these movies have on a few in the year 2270.

The other aspect of the story is the existence of human appearing androids in the year 2270, who just sit, performing a task day after day. They do not communicate other than when directed and have no personality. They are no more personable than a coffee pot, a refrigerator or a machine on an assembly line in Detroit doing the same thing day after day until they wear out.

Due to circumstances, a murderer's accomplice is arrested and thrown into a situation, where by his wits, escapes and becomes involved with two androids piloting a space ship. They are little more than electronic devices and he is a wannabe early twentieth century mobster. A good deal of the story is about their interactions, which for the most part are humorous and the possibility that in the future this interaction might occur between humans and androids.

And it is a story about their huge casino in space, the three named, Las Vegas.

CHAPTER ONE

ESCAPE WITH ANDROIDS

"Sergeant Alphonse Bruni, you have been accused of being in violation of Article 1744 of the Planetary Penal Code; The manufacture and sale of a psychedelic substance. This in itself is a serious charge, but there was a fatality associated with the sale of the contraband, involving one of your associates. The second charge being punishable by death. The Mars Constitution prohibits the intentional death of a person, so if you are tried here, we cannot carry out the penalty. For this reason, you will be transported to Earth for trial and possible conviction and punishment."

"Mr. Simpson, the accused's attorney, I have read your document in respect to the charges against your client. This is out of my hands now, tell it to the court on Earth."

Simpson asked, "Do I have to accompany Mr. Bruni to Earth?"

The judge replied, "That is unreasonable. It is a two month voyage each way. The intent is to punish Sergeant Bruni here, not you. Your client can obtain legal representation on Earth and I would assume by the military; Mr. Bruni being a sergeant in the Corp."

Al Bruni was led out of the only courthouse on Mars to the only jail on Mars. The jail having only four cells, because there was not a great deal of crime in the Mars colony of thirty thousand. Of course, both the courthouse and the jail were underground as well as almost all of the structures on mars. Almost all these structures requiring an atmosphere, were underground for obvious reasons and only the space port and agricultural fields were under their insulated glass coverings were on the surface.

Being escorted to a cell and roughly pushed into it, a cell mate named Jacob asked Al, "Well, how did that go?"

"It's good news and bad news. The bad news is that they are going to try me and execute me on Earth, and the good news is, I won't get there for three months."

Jacob replied, "Well, I wouldn't be expecting many peanuts and coffee on your trip there."

"How about you?"

"A restraining order. Apparently I'm not to frequent the Paradise Club. Something to do with the owner's wife. That's alright. They charge an arm and a leg for lime water. What did they say about that friend of yours that got killed?"

"Nothing, and he wasn't a friend, he was an associate."

Jacob said, "That's the shits. You sell someone a hit of acid and he turns around and kills you thinking you are a giant spider or something."

"That's why my end of the deal wasn't out there selling it. Most of the time its fantasy fun land, but occasionally a giant spider shows up. That idiot partner shouldn't have been hanging around for the fun part. You can't get good help anymore."

"Can they take your credits that are in the bank?"

"Oh, hell yes. They just assume it was from selling acid."

Jacob asked, "The Corp going to be your lawyers?"

Al replied, "Now that's a joke. I'll be lucky if they don't jettison me out into space on the way to Earth."

"You know most of those Corp flyboys don't you?"

"Hell, no. I worked in cargo receiving. The only thing I flew was a forklift."

Jacob replied, "Well, I'm getting out of here tomorrow, anything I can get you?"

"Yeah. A video player and a video drive with old movies."

"Lunar station stuff?"

"No, I mean *old* movies. Nineteen twenties and around there."

"Nineteen twenties?"

"Yeah. The library has every movie that was ever made."

"Why the nineteen twenties?"

"Because I was born three hundred years too late."

Jacob said, "Nineteen twenties must be cave man shit."

Al replied, "Almost."

"Ok, whatever."

James Cagney screamed from the top of the burning fuel tanks, "Top of the world, Ma," and Al had a smile on his face. He thought, *"Now that was living. Not like this shitting plastic world we have today."* He searched for Edward G Robinson and a list of movies came up and he tried to find one he hadn't watched before. Seeing nothing he hadn't watched before, he just settled for *SCARFACE* and started the movie. In his apartment, he had video drives of the best of the best movies that he had selected as his favorites, but he would never see them again. He was now limited to what Jacob had downloaded to the video drive.

After several weeks passed, Al's attorney stopped by

to tell him that a cargo vessel was leaving for Earth in a week and he would be on it. He would be confined to his quarters on the vessel and the Corp people on board were pissed. He had made them look real bad and rumor was going around that some of the Corp people were in on his little drug scheme.

Al said, "Oh, great. This should be a fun trip. I'll probably get iced."

"What's that mean?"

"Like a slug in the back of the head."

"What's that mean?"

"Forget it. What about my credits at the reserve?"

The attorney replied, "You don't have any credits."

"I had a damned fortune in there."

"That's right, you had."

"Swell. What are the chances of me escaping when I get back on Earth?

The attorney replied, "Zero or less. The Corp had a chip surgically implanted in your skull when you joined the Corp. They know where you are twenty four seven. There's no place on Earth you could go that an eliminator missile would not hit you."

"What do I have to lose?"

"Nothing I guess. It doesn't make any difference to me. Once you are off of Mars, I'm out of the picture."

"Thanks for your concern."

The attorney asked, "You don't have any more of that acid stashed away do you? We wouldn't want it to get it into the wrong hands."

Al replied, "Meaning you would legally dispose of it, right?"

"Right."

"Well, I want a video player and a copy of this video drive on the trip to Earth. You arrange that and then we'll talk."

"You got it."

Sergeant Al Bruni sat on a bunk in a small room in the space freighter *Marathon*. There was a sink, toilet, table, two chairs, a hot plate and other miscellaneous items including an off line video player. The space freighter had cleared the planet's atmosphere and increased in speed until the freighter's nuclear rockets shut down and then there was silence.

Al thought to himself, *"Well, this is a damned mess. There are dozens of movies on this video drive and they are labeled one through thirty eight and they won't let me have a deadly weapon like a pencil. It's not like I'm going to sit down pick a movie to watch by its title, so I might as well start with number one."*

Three meals a day, although they were freeze dried packages, and a pitcher of water were dropped into the room through a chute. Al knew right off that he wasn't getting the best of a wide variety of food packaged on Mars. He laboriously fixed his meals as the two surveillance cameras in the room observed every move he made. He saved out grains of rice that were in

6

groups on the table so that he could remember the best of the movies. Sixteen grains of rice was movie number sixteen; "*OUTSIDE THE LAW.*" Three weeks into the trip, he was watching the movies with no sound and speaking the dialogue as well as he could remember it.

Al Bruni was born on Earth in the year 2235 in a place that was once called New York City. It was now known as the New York District, but still called New York City by the locals. Within the last three hundred years, the face of North America had evolved many times due to rising ocean levels, climate change and the society and the government. The New York District was now nothing like the history books described America in the twentieth century. Most of the people were nothing like the people of the twentieth century. On the surface there were no more gangsters, Tommy guns, bootleggers, and all of the other things that were present back at a time that Al thought he should have taken part in. Maybe it was his genealogy that traced back to that time and his ancestors who were in the thick of it. Maybe it was his ancestors somehow beckoning to him to come back to that time and join them. Al didn't know, but everything but that time, was a total bore.

Yes, he could visualize himself in a speakeasy with twenties music blaring and girls doing the Charleston on the tables. He with a roll of paper bills in his pocket and having his competition rubbed out. Cigar smoke and spilled whiskey and occasionally slapping a good looking blonde showgirl on the butt. It was who he was inside and his life as is, was that of a fish out of water.

Oh, he did what he could to go back to the good old days and that is why he was now sitting in a small room on the way to his punishment, which would be death. Not an unpleasant experience he had heard. Under watchful eyes and he would just drop off to sleep.

While eating what must be some kind of pasta, he thought. *"This must be an A class freighter, there are passengers on board. I must be on the C deck. I remember the rooms being about this size. There must be other people heading back for Earth, maybe I can find a way to get off with them, but I have to get out of this room before we land. I wish it had been a D class freighter without locks on the doors, but I'm sure the coppers already thought of that. I think some of these doors have magnetic locks. Pushing those damned buttons doesn't work. It must be a code of some kind. Well, I might as well plan on making my move after they let me out of this room, but those damned Corp guards will be with me. Well, I have months to think on it."*

"Oh, shit, not again. How many times am I going to bump this table? That rice is everywhere. Well, I remember some of them." As the movie started starring James Cagney, Al thought, *"James Cagney; now that*

was my old man. Meaner than hell. Little, too, like Cagney. "Public Enemy Number One." Now Cagney wasn't going to let them push him around." With this thought, Al just drifted into the movie with his lips moving to the dialogue.

A dream woke Al and he thought, *"I wonder if that would work? That door is nothing like the safe Cagney cracked in the movie and I'm sure it doesn't work anything like that safe lock with the thing Cagney turned. What the hell. Can't do it with those damned cameras on me; but hell, they surely aren't watching those cameras constantly. I'll think of something."*

"I know. I'll cover the camera watching the door wall and see what happens. Why would they be watching me? Hell, I'm not going anywhere." He covered the camera and waited two days and nothing happened. *"They won't look at the monitors unless I don't return my dishes and trash. Then they'll just watch to see how I died in here. Ok, to business. I put a glass on the door and listen. Listen for what? There's nothing to turn. All I can do is touch the glass panel with the numbers on it. What the hell."* With the glass pressed against the door and his ear to the glass, just like James Cagney did, he listened intently. Surprising to him, he could hear sounds he could not normally hear from inside the room. *"Amazing. That's how he did it. He heard the lock working somehow."* Al tapped his finger on the door

and he could distinctly hear the tap. *"Ok, let's try a number."*

He put a finger tip on number one and listened. There was a slight tick of a noise as the number one button came on. He watched the lighted button and every time the light came on, there was a slight tick. *"It's that damned light."* There were no other noises and he tried all of the numbers and each had the same slight tick as the light came on.

"Well, this is bullshit," and he sat on the edge of his bunk.

Watching the cracking of the safe again by Cagney, *"He acts like he doesn't hear anything either."* It became obvious that if there was a sound coming from the safe, or in this case the door lock mechanism, it would be barely detectable. *"I wasn't listening that hard."*

With the glass pressed against the door and as close as he could get it to the door handle, he pressed number one repeatedly listening for any variation in the noise that he was hearing. There was the same quiet rumbling that was probably the power generator and other devices on the space freighter. He listened for minutes until he became accustomed to the rhythm of the sounds and finally he said, "There it is. I'll be damned. It's like a little hum that is so faint, I might be imagining it, but it's there." His intense concentration wore him out and he lay on his bunk thinking, *"I know what I'm listening for now anyway."* After a glass of water he thought, *"Oh, shit, it's probably that light in the number humming. But then, who gives a shit, this is fun. Cagney's got nothing on me."*

After days with his ear against the drinking glass, he thought, *"All ten digits hum and some sound different than others. Not much different, but different. Well, I had better get my rice out to keep track of these. I know one thing, the door codes on all the freighters are six numbers. If six of these sound different, I'm onto something."*

Another intense two days passed and looking at his little piles of rice, he could see that five numbers sounded one way and five another. *"Well, this is bullshit."* Sitting at the table with his little piles of rice, he thought, *"The sound probably doesn't have anything to do with the unlocking of the door. I wish I had a damned pencil."*

"If it does have something to do with the lock, I need six numbers and I only have five that sound alike." After a pause and staring at the rice, *"Well, idiot, the lock code has two numbers the same in it. No shit, that's it."* His next thought was, *"Which five?"*

Now with a handful of rice on the table and a headache, Al started running the numbers. *"If I pick one group of five and just try every combination, I'll get the right sequence in between one and forty five thousand tries. Well, that's bullshit. Knowing me I would pick the wrong five anyway. I've had it. Cagney didn't know how lucky he was."*

A day of contemplation passed and Al thought, *"What if the lock mechanism takes sixty volts to open and each number in the right order added ten volts? Is that forty five thousand again? I don't know, I don't think so. I don't know what the hell I'm doing. If Cagney can open the damned thing, I can."*

Hitting the one and the other nine numbers did nothing. The two and the other nine did nothing as well. Finally a six and a three and the sound increased slightly in pitch. Al thought, *"I can't be this damned lucky."*

During the process the sound increased in pitch and after hours, six- three- nine- nine-one- seven and there was an earsplitting bang to his ear on the glass as the door popped ajar. *"You have to be shitting me,"* and Al pushed the door shut and hit a random number and the door locked.

Al laughed all of the way to his bunk and collapsed with a smile on his face. He laid there thinking, *"Them coppers don't know who they're dealing with. Now, I need a plan to get off this damned freighter when it lands. The sooner I get off before they know it the better, and then what? Metal roofs. I need to stay under metal roofs. There is now way in hell the Corp can pick up that chip in this freighter with its metal hull. It will land at one of three ports, so I had better rack my brain and try to remember the buildings around them. The underground transit is no good, they have sensors down there. I think I've been awake for days, I'll get some sleep and start on this when I get up."*

"Can you believe it, I cracked a damned safe. Probably the first one to do that in two hundred and fifty years. Damn, I wish I had a pencil. I can't remember all of this shit, but I'm not going to forget that combination."

Making an assessment of what he had in his room, he thought, *"That might work,"* and he took his mirror from the wall and laid it on the table. He rubbed the surface with a bar of soap and looked at his handy work. Breaking a well-used plastic spoon, he had somewhat of a crude stylus and made a mark on the mirror surface. It didn't jump right out at you, but he could see the line and at an angle it was more distinct yet.

Al thought, *"The Dallas Space Port."* He sat and conjured up an image in his mind of the buildings around the space port and drew them on the mirror. After a considerable amount of time, he thought, *"I know I missed some, but at least I have a lot of them."* Admiring his work, *"So what, I can't hide forever in one of those damned buildings. I have to look at this realistically. All I can do is prolonging the inevitable and then they catch me. But at least I gave them a run for their money. Well, I have to concentrate on the*

Dallas Space Port while I have the drawing."

Days passed as Al studied the mirror drawings of the three U.S. space ports. The best he could, he decided on the buildings that would be his best shot at avoiding the satellites that would show his location. Most of the Dallas District was underground because they had run out of space on the surface. What buildings that existed on the surface were made of the same composite material that all buildings were made of, which was no more than fine earth material and epoxy in any size or shape needed and as strong as steel. But it wasn't metal and prying sensors saw right through it. In the old days, when there were metal automobiles, he would at least have a shot at getting away from the space ports, but the moving walkways were all out in the open or only covered with glass canopies. It passed through his mind, *"If we get there during daylight, the tramways will be packed with people and that might help. The coppers probably won't even scan for me until they know I've escaped. If I can get under cover before they scan, it will be like I just disappeared. Maybe they will think the crew just deep sixed me out into space on the way. What would George Raft do in this situation; he was the smart cunning gangster? This orange jumpsuit. What in the hell am I going to do about that? Nothing works in an orange jumpsuit. And I need a damned pencil or pen and some paper. I need some clothes and some maps of the three spaceports. Hell, they are already screwed up in my head. If I'm on C deck, I know where I can get both, but it's risky. There are eight crewmen on board unless things have changed. Six on one shift and one on the other two. When there is only one, they have to stay on the bridge. I have to chance getting the stuff on one of those shifts. I can't tell by the food drop because that's all automated. Maybe if I listen with the glass, I can tell."*

Watching movies with the sound off and his ear pressed to the drinking glass, he determined what shift had the crew of six on board by the increase in noise. He synchronized that with the feeding drops and had somewhat of a clock.

Six-three-nine-nine-one-seven and the door popped ajar. Listening at the gap, Al waited several minutes and stuck his head out the door. "Yep, section C. Removing his synthetic slippers and in his sock feet, he made a dash down the hall and made a left down another hall, then a right and stopped at a door that he opened quickly. Inside there were racks with an assortment of materials on them. Pen, paper, Corp uniforms, caps, synthetic shoes and he was out of there and back in his room in just minutes. He passed one surveillance camera, but could only hope no one was watching.

"Now we're cooking with bacon grease. I had better hide this uniform and the shoes. Then I think I'll have a

cup of mud and relax." Pouring a cup of hot water, Al sat at the table staring at the notebook in front of him. *"I have the New York Spaceport on the mirror, so I might as well do it first, but much more detailed and see if I can find a route to get out of town. Why? Hell, I don't know, you have to have something to shoot at. The mobster Robinson always had the law looking for him and he got away. It was always one of his buddies that plugged him, and I don't have any buddies."*

Looking at his drawing of the New York District Space Port, Al thought, *"Well, there's a lot of blank spaces here, but I was there only a week loading a freighter. The Space Terminal has a metal roof for sure; I can remember hail hitting it. There are dozens of small private space liners always lined up there. I would try to steal one if I knew how to operate the damned thing. It's only a half mile to the terminal. If I run my ass off, I can probably get there before I'm missed. The terminal is at least a mile long and on the pedestrian tramway I can go the length of the terminal in ten minutes. Cross the fifth street tramway and into the Federal Building. I'm sure they have some type of anti-hacking shielding built right into the building. I would have to find somewhere in there to hold up for a few days and that won't be easy."*

"Ok, Cape Canaveral Space Port. If the freighter sits down there, I'm screwed. Nothing there but launch sites and a high speed rail line you have to have

identification to get on and its crawling with coppers. I'm not even going to waste my time on it. If it lands there I'll just go have a beer in that fancy tourist's lounge. A beer I can't pay for and wait."

A plan was made for the Dallas location and a couple weeks to fine tune the plans, Al just ran them through his mind every day and watched his movies thinking he might pick up some pointers from people on the lam. "I don't even have a rod. Hell, there hasn't been one around for a hundred years. Some gangster on the run I'm going to be. No rod, no bankroll, no nothing."

Sitting up in bed, he thought, "The chip is in the top of my head. If I had a piece of metal on my head, that would shield the satellite detectors. Yeah, but what about the detectors on the street? A metal pot would work." Al laughed and thought, "Now wouldn't that be a sight. The coppers could just go to where all of the people were laughing. James Cagney with a metal pot on his head. We're talking sacrilegious stuff here. Well, it was a thought. I figure I have about a snowballs chance in hell on this deal, but if nothing else, I will die knowing I cracked a safe and I'm not going to tell them how I did it. It'll drive them nuts."

All of his options ran through his head day and night and there were few. His drawings were imprinted in his mind and keeping from being caught was a matter of timing and dumb luck. Cape Canaveral kept going through his mind as his third option and it never looked more favorable than impossible. The Cape was now a man-made island two miles offshore due to the sea level rise and there was an underground rail line out to the cape that for the most part carried freight for the space freighters. Due to a variety of problems at the Cape, security was extreme. Facial recognition and of course Corp monitoring of their people with chip implants. If by a miracle he got on the bullet train, he would never get off on the other end. It didn't really matter where the freighter landed, it was just a matter of time until he was caught, but he sure as hell didn't want to get caught in thirty minutes.

"I have no idea in hell when this thing will get to Earth; but when we get close, I'll be able to tell by the rocket thrust to slow this baby down. Then, thirty minutes to touchdown. They might check the cameras once to see how I'm doing down here, so I had better play it cool. Hell, I can dress in thirty seconds."

Al couldn't tell when they turned the ship around because it was such a slow maneuver, but there was a slight trembling as the thruster rockets increased in force. The artificial gravity system on the ship that was normally eighty percent of normal gravity was changing and the gravity effect was picking up and it felt like he weighed a ton. He had made enough freighter landings that he could tell by the gravity effect when the ship was going to touch down.

"One minute to go. Six-three-nine-nine-one seven."
The door came ajar and Al hurriedly put on the Corp uniform and glancing in the mirror, he looked like any other Corp private. A demotion, but that was ok. He had memorized the route from his cabin to the freight door of F Deck that would automatically open on touchdown. There would be Corp people there with forklifts and other equipment to unload the freighter, but to them he would just be one of the freighter's crew.

He ran down several flights of stairs to the freight door and it was half open when he arrived. He looked down at the ground with his cap bill covering his face and when the door slammed open, he walked straight out on to the launch pad loading dock, seeing nothing but legs as he walked by the Corp people.

"CAPE CANAVERAL SPACE PORT"

"Shit, shit, shit, shit. Wouldn't you know it? Screw it. I have to get into the terminal building quick."
When in the terminal building and walking as fast as he could without attracting attention, he glanced at the signs looking for some indication of somewhere he could hide.

The PA system was blaring as he walked and it was stating take off times for the Moon for the benefit of Corp people going on the Moon freighters. There being a million people on the moon, it required a lot of freighters. As he hurried by he could see flashing signs like Freighter 2010, departure two hours twenty four minutes. Another, freighter 4223, departure six hours, nineteen minutes. Al saw the sign ahead, CAPE CANAVERAL BULLET TRAIN, ahead five exits. Already he could see coppers standing around in their red uniforms and more ahead in the direction of the bullet train. *"Freighter 2772 departure in five minutes."*

"The coppers will be watching for me on their monitors at anytime. Hell, the sensors are everywhere in here."

FREIGHTER 2772 LOADING DOCK. *"Screw it, I have to get out of here,"* and he headed out the door and stepped behind a forklift heading for the big freighter. The driver had no idea Al was behind him and when at the freighter door the fork lift turned around to back in and Al stayed behind the fork lift and then ran through the freighter door. There was another forklift stacking cargo, but didn't see Al and he ran behind a massive stack of freight boxes and hid. *"Well, ass hole, you're headed for the moon. That will buy you a day anyway until you get there. At least there is probably very little surveillance there, no satellites and everything underground. If I had any credits I would be feeling good about this, but I don't. Maybe I can find a job off the books somewhere. It's worth a shot. The downside is that I know they can execute you on the moon. That's the U.S.'s preferred place to do it."*

The freight door closed and he had seen a lot of

activity in the windows of the terminal with red dressed coppers running everywhere.

The rumble increased in volume and Al felt the gravitational effect of getting heavier and he sat on a box to give his legs a break. In fifteen minutes he was in near zero gravity as the gravity simulator increased and he was back up to his accustomed eighty percent gravity.

"*I'm starved,*" and he started looking through the cargo expecting to see potatoes, carrots and other vegetables, but settled for a can of corned beef and a packet of apple juice. "*Well, I have a day, so I might as well get some rest,*" and he lay between boxes and went to sleep.

Waking, he had some more corned beef and thought, "*This is going to be a long day without my video player. I have the video drive and no player, that's about right. I haven't heard a sound; I might as well look around for something to do. They aren't wasting any power on lights down here and it's starting to get cold. They won't freeze the food in here though. There must be enough in here for the moon for days. Almost all canned meat it looks like. Well, it beats the hell out of that crap I ate for months.*" Al wandered around what was marked F Deck for a while and was surprised by the sound of a door slamming behind him. "*Oh, shit, the jig is up,*" and he turned slowly to see an android no more than twenty feet from him walking directly at him. Not knowing what to do, he said, "Private Miller," and the android looked him in the eyes for but a second and walked right by him. *"He must think I'm part of the crew."* The android stopped in the middle of F Deck and looked at every box and container. He turned and walked back towards Al and stopped just before getting to him, and Al thought, *"Oh, shit,"* as the android looked at the empty corned beef can on a box next to Al. The android seemed to take note of it and then continued on and out the door.

Al mumbled, "He's going to rat me out. I had better keep an eye on him," and Al went through the door in time to see the android turn down a hallway and continued following him. The hallways were short and then they went up the stairs to E Deck. The android took note of all of the cargo there and then Al followed him to D Deck and so on until they were on B Deck. Still following down short hallways, Al passed a doorway and another android stood just inside watching him. *"Well, shit."* The two stood staring at each other and then the android walked past him and headed in the same direction as the first android.

"In for a penny, in for a pound," and Al followed his new acquaintance. They walked by the crews quarters and mess hall and he thought, *"They must all be on the bridge."*

Curiosity getting the best of him, when they arrived at the door to the bridge on A Deck, the android entered and Al went to the door and slowly and quietly opened a crack big enough he could see the entire bridge and he whispered, "That's it? Two androids on the whole damned Freighter. *I heard there were freighters with only androids. Hell, they know I'm not part of the crew, there isn't a crew. Maybe I can get them to keep their mouth shut about me before we get to the moon. They seemed like nice enough guys.*" Al entered the bridge and got a glance from both of the androids and then they ignored him. He sat next to the two at the large ships control panel and he said, "Hi boys, how's it going?" This got another glance and that was it.

"Well, so much for small talk. I'll let them come to me. They must be wondering what in the hell I'm doing onboard."

The androids kept busy as Al sat there and after several hours, Al said, "I'm going down to the mess hall, you boys need anything?" He didn't even get a glance at this. *"Well, no news is good news,"* and Al *went to the mess hall and microwaved a Salisbury steak dinner. "This isn't too bad, good food and good company."* After a half pot of real coffee, Al went back to the bridge and the two androids were in the same seats. There was no communications between them, but they seemed to be working on something together.

Al thought, *"Wi-Fi. They know I'm here, but they just ignore the fact. That's better than getting wrestled to the ground and handcuffed I guess. Someone did a miserable job on these guys. It looks like they both had a bad cosmetic surgery job. It's nice that they are wearing uniforms though, but I'm curious what they have down below."*

On one of the monitors, some numbers appeared and images of what appeared to be freight boxes. Below each was universal computer text indicating what was in them and the quantity. A couple items were deleted and boxes moved around on the monitors and the two androids continued watching the monitors.

"They are doing that, Wi-Fi, I guess. I wonder if I can get online with them?" Al scooted up to a keyboard and synchronized the monitor XX17 in front of him. Using universal computer language, he typed in, "Hello, my name is Al."

The androids instantly looked at him and on his monitor was the reply, "You are not on the manifest."

Al replied, "No, I am on a quality control mission for the Space Port."

An instant reply on Al's monitor read, *"Everything is accounted for here, except one can of corned beef. That falls in the area of acceptable loss, but we know it is still a violation. We will report it."*

From Al, *"Why don't you take a can of corned beef from the mess hall and put it in the freight and then there will be no loss to report?"*

The androids looked at each other, a number was changed on the monitor and then there was the text, *"There is no loss."* One of the androids then got up and headed for the mess hall.

Al thought, *"This might come in handy,"* as he watched the surveillance camera monitors as the android made his way from B Deck to F Deck and back. *"The side hallways are the blind spots."*

With both androids now back on the bridge in their seats and obviously communicating back and forth, Al typed in, *"If you can speak, do you speak English?"*

The monitor said, *"We can vocalize and we speak some of eighty-five languages."*

"What does some amount to?"

Al's monitor read, *"DANGER, FIRE, EVACUATE."*

"That's it?"

"Yes, in eighty five different languages."

"Will you say these for me?"

"Is there a fire, danger, or we need to evacuate?"

"No."

"Then we can't."

Al typed, *"Will you say Mess hall?"*

"Is it on fire?"

"No."

"Then why would we say it?"

"I need to test your alarms."

Within one second both of the Androids yelled "Fire," that almost burst Al's ear drums and surely could be heard in the entire freighter.

Al thought, *"My God,"* and typed *"Can you reduce the volume?"*

"Yes."

"Reduce the volume and we will test the low

decibels."

"Fire," was yelled by both and still loud, but at least not lethal.

"That's fine. Your audio is working. Keep it at low decibels because there is no one to warn but me and I am right here."

"Volume reduced."

Al thought for a minute and typed, *"How many hours to the moon?"*

A number flashed on the monitor and Al just stared at it. *"There's some mistake, they must not have understood the question."*

Again, *"How many hours travel time to the moon?"*

"The same number appeared, *"2,880.4."*

"Hours to the moon?"

"Yes, hours to the moon."

"That's the hours to the Moon?"

"No."

"That's what I thought."

A new number flashed on the monitor, *"2,880.3 hours to the moon."*

Al said to the androids in English, "That's bullshit," and he typed in *"Let's see your flight path."*

On the screen was an astronomical map with a route on it and it said, *"Earth to Mars, Mars to the Moon, Moon to earth."*

"Mars? I can't go to Mars."

On the monitor, *"You are going to Mars. We do not know your schedule."*

Al said out loud, "My schedule is, I'm screwed and I am looking at sitting in a shithole cabin for the next four months and then executed."

On the monitor it said, "*We do not understand your vocalization.*"

Al typed, "*Has the Earth contacted you?*"

"*The Earth communicates with the ship's computer, not us.*"

"*Never?*"

"*Never.*"

"*Does the surveillance video go to Earth?*"

"*Yes.*"

"*Well, shit. So much for hiding from the coppers. Do you two use the Captains Quarters?*"

"*What for?*"

"*That's where I'll be.*"

The monitor said, "*That's of no interest to us unless you start a fire.*"

"*Ah, a sixty five inch monitor. Now we're talking. A cushioned bed, coffee, good food, no surveillance cameras, the whole ball of wax. I would be proud of myself if I had planned this gig. A four month stay of execution. Now, something has to go wrong, what is it? What are the possibilities? They can't turn this freighter around. All they can do is just wait for me at Mars. Unless, they communicate with the androids and have them lock me up in a closet somewhere on bread and water and no movies. That's what they'll do, they are probably pissed at me getting away. More likely yet, they will just have the androids eject me into space and say they have no idea what happened to me after I got to earth. I'm going to raid the mess hall and load this room up and lock the door. That Captain's door is one they're not going to get through."*

Now with a clock, he could see that three days had passed since he had been on the bridge and he had heard nothing from the androids. *"They probably sit in those same damned chairs for months; it's not like they have to eat or go take a leak. What a boring son of a bitch that would be. Who am I to talk, that's all I've been doing for a year. Those two are probably broke, too. Well, play the hand you're dealt, Cagney said. I might as well go see if they have heard anything from the coppers."*

Al entered the bridge making as much noise as he could and the two androids acted like they didn't even know he was on the same space freighter and that continued as he sat next to them. "Hello, you two," and there was no reaction and then he typed on the keyboard, *"Hello, you two,"* and still nothing. Well, if I'm getting anything out of them, I'll have to ask a question. He typed, *"Is everything ship shape, boys?"*

The two looked at each other and the monitor said, *"Yes, it only has one shape."*

"Is everything in order?"

"Yes. What's boys?"

"Two androids sitting on the bridge."

The reply was, *"What if there was just one android sitting on the bridge?"*

"That would be boy."

"The S means two boys?"

"Yes."

Another reply, *"Why don't you say two boy?"*

"Cancel this topic."

"Ok."

Al asked, *"Anything from earth?"*

"How would we get anything from earth?"

"I mean, have they contacted you with a communication?"

"They don't communicate with us, they communicate with the spaceship's computer. That is not our job."

Al typed, *"Has Earth communicated with the spaceships computer?"*

"Yes."

"Well?"

"Well, what?"

"What was the communication?"

"We don't know, it was not for us."

Al thought, *"My God. I might as well be talking to myself."* Typing, *"What do you androids do on this ship?"*

The monitor said, *"We get it to Mars and correct any malfunctions on the way. If the ship cannot control itself, we control it."*

"You fly the spaceship?"

"If necessary."

"Have you ever had to fly a spaceship?"

"No."

"You boys like movies?"

"What is like and what is movies?"

Al thought, *"You boys are going to be a lot of fun. A movie is a video image of a story."*

"What's a story?"

"Like if you had a video of your last trip to watch."

The monitor read, *"A two month long video?"*

"Oh, my, God." *"No, it was condensed down to an hour."*

"Why don't we condense this trip down to an hour and the trip will be over?"

"Oh my God, I thought my drug dealing partner was dumb." "Do you boys want to watch a movie?"

"For an hour?"

"Yes, an hour."

"Yes. We want to see two months condensed to an hour. Will it be a blur?"

"No, but it's in the English language."

The monitor said, *"That will not be a problem; the computer will translate it into computer language."*

"It can do that?"

"Where are you from, New York?"

Al replied, *"Yes. I'll go get my video drive."*

At a run, Al was off to the captain's quarters and

back with his video disk. He handed it to one of the androids and Al typed in, *"Can we get it on all three monitors?"*

The reply was, *"Yes. On yours it will be audio video and ours it will be video with captions in computer language."*

"Suits me."

"You said the audio is in English?"

"Yes."

Adjusting some controls, the video came onto all three monitors, *"THE ROARING TWENTIES,"* Starring *James Cagney and Humphrey Bogart."*

Two minutes into the movie, Al looked at the two androids like a new father showing his baby in the maternity ward. There was no reaction from the androids of course and Al concentrated on the movie with his lips moving with the dialogue. Twenty minutes into the movie the picture froze and on top of it was text overlaid by the androids. *"The computer says that most of the dialogue is not in English."*

Irritated at the interruption of the movie and the disrespect shown by the androids, Al typed in *"Bullshit."*

"What is bullshit, the name of the movie?"

"Well, I can see the movie is way over you two's heads."

"It's not over our heads, its right there in front of us."

Al replied, *"Ok, shut the damned thing off."*

One of the androids typed, "*I want to see what happens to the baby human.*"

A red faced Al yelled, "That's not a baby human, it's James Cagney" and typed, "*Go ahead and watch the damned thing.*"

Al's monitor read, "*The computer cannot interpret the movie language, so it has left the text not interpreted blank. I'm not going to watch a movie where half the text is blank. So far it has been meaningless.*"

Al typed, "*For Christ's sake, what words didn't it understand?*"

"*The computer listed them, look on my monitor.*"

"*Ok,*" and Al slid his chair next to the android and on the screen came the message, "*That's not my monitor.*"

Getting up, Al walked to the other android's seat and looked at the monitor and the android typed, "*This is the list,*" and the screen filled with; "*Tommy gun, john law, Billy club, joint, stool pigeon, G-man, racket, dough, bum rap, slug, flatfoot, heater, copper, a ride, bump off, bracelets, booze, broad, punk, squeal, mouth piece, spill tha beans, frisk, job, brass knuckles, tha pen, in tha can.*"

Back at his seat, Al typed, "*You're shitting me. You watched this movie for twenty minutes with all of those words blanked out?*"

"*What's shitting me, mean?*"

"*What a couple goof balls.*"

"What's a goof ball?"

"Aw, horse shit, I might as well be cooped up with a couple first graders."

"What's cooped up mean?"

Al yelled it, then typed, *"Print me out that damned list and I'll type and print out the definitions."*

"Can we watch the rest of the movie?"

"Why?"

"I want to see what happens to that baby human?"

Al typed, *"Aw, horse shit; go ahead. Amazing, you know what horse shit is."*

"Yes, but I don't know how it applies to this situation."

"Swell. I'm going to use the computer in the captain's quarters and I will send the definitions to this monitor, XX17."

"Why am I doing this? Is there a chance in hell those two could appreciate just how good that movie is? That one android kind of liked it, and I don't know which one it was. Maybe they have an inkling of a personality. How in the hell would I know. Well, when you are on a two month trip right into the mouth of a dragon, you have to not think about the dragon. Beats the shit out of that last two months. I wonder if they will understand the lingo after I do all of this? Oh, oh, I had better add lingo to the list."

When Al got back to the bridge, the movie had

finished and the two were checking surveillance camera images assumedly looking for a fire or other problems.

"*You boys understand that gangster lingo now?*"

"*What's gangster lingo?*"

"*Don't sweat it, it's on the list.*"

"*We don't sweat. That's an animal function.*"

"*Oh, shit. Ok, don't sweat it will be on there too.*" Al added a few more terms and words to the list and as the updated list and definitions came up on the android's monitors and the androids studied them, Al could see that they were chatting back and forth as well.

Al's monitor showed, "*I thought it was going to make some sense. We understand the definitions for the lingo, but why did they use a term that they knew wasn't correct?*"

"*It was gang slang. Oh, shit, I know, what's gang slang?*"

The monitor said, "*I know; a poem?*"

Al yelled in English, "You two don't know shit," and he typed, "*Do you want to watch a damned movie with the translations or not?*"

"*I do. I want to see the baby human die again. I don't know why he died. The other human pointed something at him that smoked and he fell over.*"

Al replied, "*That was a rod, it shoots a projectile that killed him. You two shut up and watch the movie again without picking it to pieces.*"

"*How do you pick a movie to pieces?*"

Al activated the movie and left the bridge thinking.

"I've about had a gut full of those two."

Al couldn't help himself, he had to go see what the movie critics thought of the movie the second time through. When he entered the bridge, the two androids were again doing their normal duties, whatever that was. Al sat at his monitor and typed, *"Well, what do you think?"*

The reply was, *"Where is that place?"*

"New York City."

"That's not New York City, I have been there."

"My God man, that was about three hundred years ago."

"You might have mentioned that to us."

"Well I'm sorry, I thought you could figure that out."

Al's monitor said, *"How could we figure that out? We thought it was on an asteroid."*

"An asteroid? You're kidding me, why?"

"It wasn't Earth, Mars or the Moon."

"Ok. It was three hundred years ago on Earth, before androids and computers. What did you think?"

On the monitor came, *"Interesting,"* and below that came, *"Do you have any more movies?"*

"There are thirty seven or thirty eight on that video disk I made."

"Are they different movies?"

"No knuckleheads, there are thirty seven more of the same movie."

"Knuckleheads?"

"Forget it. Do you two have names?"

"If you mean identification. I am Model RTR, Serial Number137554."

"And I am Model RTR, Serial Number 137555."

Al typed, *"You over there with the red dot on your forehead, you're Ace, and you right here with the blue spot, you're Legs."*

"I don't want to be, Legs."

"Too bad, you're, Legs."

The reply was, *"Well then, you're Foot."*

"Fine. I don't want to be Foot, but I'm Foot. Are you happy?"

"No, I'm not Happy, you said I was Legs not Happy."

"Foot? Ace here. Let's watch another movie."

"Really?"

"Androids don't lie."

"LITTLE CAESER," staring Edward G Robinson."

One minute into the movie, Ace asked, *"Foot, where is the baby human?"*

"He is not in this movie."

"I know that. He got killed. Did they just leave him lying on the street?"

"Shut up and watch this movie."

Twenty minutes into the movie, Legs asked, *"Why don't the humans fall down when they get shot?"*

Al answered, *"They missed."*

"What do you mean miss?"

"The slug didn't hit the human."

"Then what's the point of shooting the rod?"

"Watch the movie, Legs. When it's over I'll spend a week explaining it to you."

"That complicated, huh?"

"Do you think we could cut the chatter until the movie is over?"

"Cut the chatter?"

"THE END," and Ace asked, *"Do all movies end with the gangster crawling down the street and dying?"*

"Usually, yes."

"If I was going to make a movie, I would have him get killed at the beginning of the movie and then the rest of the movie would explain why and how."

Al replied, *"The people watching the movie don't want the guy to get killed. Why would they watch the movie? They think he might not get killed."*

"That's reasonable."

Legs interrupted, *"I bet I can tell which ones get killed before the end of the movie."*

Ace replied, *"How could you do that? The guy with the gun might do what Foot says. He missed."*

"That's true. They miss an unreasonable amount of times."

"So there is no way to know."

"Foot?"

"Yes, Legs?"

"What do they do with all of the dead people to make a movie? Do they have a place to bury these people?"

"Give me a break. These are actors, they don't die, they just pretend to die."

"Well, baby human looked dead to me?"

"If you see another movie with James Cagney in it, will you accept that they are just pretending?"

Legs answered, *"Yes. Have you heard of; what's the moral of the story?"*

"Certainly."

"Well, what was the moral of that last story?"

Al replied, *"If you live by the sword, you die by the sword."*

"I see that and I will consider that."

"You do that. You don't communicate with Earth, right?"

"No, the computer does."

"Do you know what these communications are?"

Legs replied, *"If we wanted to, but we have never wanted to."*

Al said, *"Well, for the fun of it, can you tell me what the communications have been?"*

"How could that be fun?"

"Ok, interesting."

Legs and Ace manipulated their keyboards and Legs, replied to Al. *"There has only been one communication out of protocol. The Earth Spaceport had a request. The request was to enable all of the surveillance cameras and transmit the video and audio to them in real time."*

"Are there any cameras on the bridge?"

"There are no cameras on the bridge and the rest of A Deck"

"Then I would be on video transmitted to earth when I was on the other decks?"

"Yes. It would be transmitted at some time."

Ace asked, *"Why are you concerned, you work for them don't you?"*

"Yes. I just want them to know I got safely onboard. Well, its bedtime for me."

Legs typed, *"What about the next movie?"*

"Just watch one more."

"Ok."

Looking at the captain's quarter's clock, Al could see that he had slept over ten hours and thought, *"At least I know how long I slept. That's refreshing. I'm thinking scrambled eggs and sausage this morning. I guess its morning somewhere. I wonder how the boys are doing on the bridge. I'll bet you two bits they are still in those same damned chairs. Now you talk about boring. They don't eat, they don't sleep, they don't go take a crap and they don't have anything to look forward too. On the bright side, they aren't going to be executed in four months. I wonder if there is any booze in that freight. It's illegal on Mars, but a little money greases the wheel on Earth and I bet on Mars too. Hell, I know those Mars politicians party. Being quality control for the Space Port, it won't hurt to ask if there is any booze on board. Hell, it's my duty."*

At his chair at the console, *"Good morning boys, how is it going?"*

"It is not morning in Cape Canaveral. We are now on Cape Canaveral time."

"Well, excuse me. How was the movie?"

Legs typed, *"I have a question."*

"Shoot."

"I don't want to shoot you, I just want to ask a question."

Ace added, *"Legs doesn't have a rod."*

"What's the damned question?"

Legs asked, *"What does cracking a safe mean?"*

Al replied, *"You have heard of cracking the door a little?"*

"Yes."

"Same thing. Open the door."

Legs replied, *"It doesn't take me twenty minutes to open a door and I never rub the handle."*

"That was Smiley in the movie?"

"Yes."

"Well, he's not very smart."

"Obviously."

Al asked, *"Any word from Earth?"*

"Why would they send me a word?"

"Have they communicated with the computer?"

Ace replied, *"They never stop communicating."*

"Anything out of the ordinary?"
"No."

CHAPTER TWO

MOON SHINE

The three sat motionless for a while and Al typed, *"Is there any booze on the freighter?"*

"No."

"Maybe some you don't know about?"

Legs replied, *"If there is some I don't know about, how could I say I know about it? I should have said I wouldn't know, but it's my job to know."*

"Ok, ok, I get it, I get it."

"How could you get it, you don't know if there is any on board."

After a brief silence, Al said. *"I am supposed to*

check the medical supplies."

Ace said, *"Why, we already did that?"*

"Is there any alcohol in the medical supplies?"

"Yes. There are two hundred twenty seven drugs on board with alcohol in them."

"No pure alcohol then?"

"No."

"Well, shit. Are there any good computer games on this computer?"

"Yes, for the ship's crew."

Al asked, *"How do I access them on the captain's quarters computer?"*

Legs typed in, *"Ace you explain it to him, it may take a week, I'm busy."*

On Al's monitor the text came up, *"Hit games."*

Al typed, *"No movie for eight hours for that, smart asses."*

Three days passed an   Al was in the captain's quarters and playing a build your own planet game and he thought, *"What I would really like is a cold beer to wash down this popcorn. I haven't had a cold beer since my last post on Earth. That was at least five years ago. In the old part of Manhattan, what's left of it. It's hard to believe they poured all of the floors of those buildings that are now partially underwater full of concrete. Boat City, they call it now. A few floating bridges and a million electric boats. I wonder where they got the beer in Manhattan. Probably Milwaukee*

District or somewhere like that. How in the hell do you make beer? It's nearly all water. Hell, those bootleggers made it by the millions of gallons in downtown Chicago. It must not be brain surgery. Maybe I could make some here in my room, I have water. Google it I guess."

Al was on his computer for the better part of two days researching the making of beer. He had time for a couple movies with the boys and all of the nonsense that went along with watching the movies. He thought, *"And those two are flying a space ship."*

He had a list of the ingredients needed to make a basic beer and the only things in his quarters that were on the list were water and sugar, and not enough sugar. *"There may be some of the ingredients down in the freight, but there was no way in hell the androids are going to let me steal any of the freight."* He didn't know what they would do, but he saw one of them easily move a five hundred pound box. Hell, he could never find it anyway. The androids would have to tell him where what he was looking for was located. *"I'm going to have to trick them. With those two, that shouldn't be too hard."*

On the computer, *"What day is it Legs?"*

"April nineteenth."

"That's what I thought. On the nineteenth I have to start preparing for the test."

"What test?"

"Like the one for you two and the can of corned beef."

Ace replied, "That was a test?"

"Yes. To see if you were going to report it. You were, so you passed the security test."

Legs said, "Well, actually we didn't report it."

"I know, because I told you it wasn't necessary. You had already passed the test."

"You are giving us another test?"

Al replied, "Oh, hell no. This is for receiving on the other end. On Mars. Freight has come up missing and when some was missing it wasn't being reported."

"Oh, I see."

"I need to take something from the freight. Several items at random and hide them in my quarters until the freight is offloaded on Mars."

Ace said, "This is a setup, then."

"Yes, a setup."

Legs said, "And we are not supposed to rat you out when we get to Mars."

"Exactly. Pull up the freight inventory and I'll buzz through it, just for something to do. I have plenty of time."

"Buzz through it? You aren't going to damage it are you?"

"Oh, hell no. I'll keep a perfect record of the items I take. I have to if it goes to court."

Ace said, "Well, get a judge on the take."

"*I will.*"

The inventory came up on the monitor, or some of it did, because there were hundreds of pages.

"*You boys haven't watched "DOORWAY TO HELL" yet, have you?*"

"*No.*"

"*I'll put it on, while I buzz through the inventory.*"

"*Ok.*"

With the movie on the android's monitors, Al searched for dry malt extract and it popped right up under Bakery. Yeast was an issue because there were at least a dozen different types, so he picked one that sounded like it would go in beer. Corn syrup was not a problem, but it was in thirty five gallon drums. He searched hops and the search said "*Zero,*" for hops. "*Horse shit. I don't know much about beer, but I know they all have hops in it.*" A quick Google and the results were that hops were bitter. "*Ok, a substitute. What is bitter on this damned list?*"

With the androids glued to the monitors, Al searched bitter and a lot of things were bitter, but not on the inventory list. "*Alum, that's it. Cooking Alum. I heard Alum was bitter, but I thought it was poison. It says this type isn't and it's bitter. Close enough, it doesn't take much. I need more sugar. Now barley. Shit, nothing on barley. Thousands of pounds of freeze dried wheat and no barley, that figures. Well, wheat it is. Beer doesn't taste like barley anyway.*" Al noted the locations of his selected ingredients, deck, box number and so on. *"Now I need some big metal containers, or plastic. Whatever. There should be some in the crew's laundry room. A hydrometer from sick bay. And a thermometer."*

The movie ended and Legs typed, *"Well, that was the shits."*

Al replied, *"You didn't like it?"*

"I thought he was going to get away. He would have if that Smiley character hadn't ratted him out."

"I'm through with your inventory list. I had the computer pick some things at random."

Ace asked, *"What are they?"*

"I can't tell you, security you know. It's security protocol. I will give you the list after the freight is off loaded, so your numbers will check out."

Ace replied, *"We will know what they are because you will be on surveillance cameras."*

"Oh, you'll have to turn them off while I get the items."

"What about Earth monitoring the cameras?"

"Oh they know. They don't want someone on their end tipping people off on Mars."

Legs replied. *"Sounds copacetic to me."*

"I'll get the goods tomorrow. I have to go do my laundry today. You boys need anything laundered?"

"Why would we need anything laundered?"

"You wouldn't, I guess."

In the laundry room, Al found two large blue plastic tubs that had been used for who knows what. He washed them out, making sure there was no lingering soap in them. With these in the room drying, he again went over the beer recipe and the locations of all of the ingredients in the freight in the decks below.

The next morning, or what Al considered the next morning, he entered the bridge and walked to his monitor and keyboard. *"Is it morning in Cape Canaveral?"*

"Yes."

"Well, good morning then. How was the movie?"

"A little repetitious, and I have some more words and phrases for your definitions."

"Fine. Right after I go get the items out of freight. You can go ahead and turn off the surveillance cameras now. I'll let you know when I'm finished."

"Ok."

"F Deck, box 134, malt extract. Might as well start at the bottom and work up." Al made his way to F Deck that had the large freight door where he had entered the ship and he searched for box 134. Finding it, the boxes were actually vacuum sealed plastic and he had to look for a tool box to get something to cut the plastic. Cutting a hole in box 134, he reached in and pulled out four boxes of freeze dried malt extract. *"Sugar, box 337."* Finding the sugar, he acquired a

twenty pound bag of sugar. And so it went until he was in his quarters exhausted. The twenty pound sack of sugar had just about done him in.

"I had better check in with the knuckleheads so they can get the cameras back on. No need to make them suspicious."

Al typed, *"Ok boys, I'm done. You can turn the cameras back on."*

The surveillance monitors lit up and Legs said, *"Earth contacted the computer and asked why the cameras were off."*

"Well?"

"The computer replied to Earth that it would run an analysis. That's it. Nothing more about the cameras."

Al said, *"Earth is checking the ships security diagnostics?"*

"That's what we concluded."

"How about a movie. Try number twenty three, "ANGELS AND DIRTY FACES."

"ANGELS AND DIRTY FACES?" *"What kind of a title is that? If it was any longer you wouldn't have to watch the movie."*

"Ok, smart ass. Call it anything you want."

"How could I name it if I haven't even seen it?"

"Start the damned movie."

Ace asked, *"Who is the actor?"*

Al replied, *"Your favorite, James Cagney."*

"I hope he isn't going to start crying again."

Al watched the movie, but the thought of a cold beer made him lose his concentration. Legs and Ace were watching it like manikins, but on occasion they would look at each other and Al could almost hear their thought, "*What does that mean?*"

The instant the movie was over and before a long argument could ensue, Al typed a message over the movie credits; "*I have to get some sleep. I'll see you boys in the morning, or afternoon, or whatever.*"

He stood and left the bridge and walked to the captain's quarters and looked over the loot he had acquired from the freight down below. Following the beer recipe, he filled the plastic tubs with ten gallons of warm water each and added the ingredients of the recipe. It looked terrible with the freeze dried wheat floating on top and it popped into Al's mind, "*Shit, the freeze dried wheat will absorb the water. I have to allow for the water the wheat absorbs and add that much more.*"

It still looked terrible, but he put lids on the tubs and thought, "*All there is to do now is wait.*"

Al crawled into his bed with visions of cold beers in front of him as he visualized sitting at a scratched up bar in old Chicago.

When he awoke, he lifted a lid on one of the tubs and his concoction looked the same, other than the wheat grains had increased a little in size and some had sank. With a hot sausage microwaved breakfast in hand, he walked to the bridge and entered to the same sight he saw every time he opened the door. After sitting at his monitor and not getting a look from either android, he typed, *"Ok, where are the new words?"*

Words and phrases appeared on the monitor and Al added the definitions for them and said, *"If you two could speak English this would all be a lot easier."*

"We can speak English."

"Yeah, but I have to light a fire to hear it."

"We can speak all English words," was on the monitor.

"I don't want to ask this, but what does that mean?"

In perfect English, Legs said, "We can speak all of the English words. Ever since we watched the first movie."

Al yelled, "You mean to tell me we have been going through this computer monitor bullshit for weeks for nothing?"

"You said that was what you wanted to do."

"Well, kiss my ass."

"We do not have that human emotion."

Ace, also in English, said, "What does knuckle heads mean? It's not in the movies?"

"Just a complimentary term used for androids."

"Well, thank you."

"Enough of this bullshit. I'll be in my quarters reading some old books on the computer."

Ace asked, "Are you studying for a test?"

"No, history books."

"About bank heists and scores like that?"

"Exactly. Watch all of those movies you want, you might learn something."

Legs asked, "Do you have any skin flicks?"

"No, why?"

"Just curious."

"You wouldn't like them, trust me."

Back in his quarters, Al checked his brew and there wasn't a noticeable difference. There was that almost sickening smell of malt, but within hours he didn't notice it that much.

"That wasn't a bad idea, reading history books. Something different anyway and a watched pot never boils. That beer is going to take its old sweet time."

He was in the room for three days and the temperature he had to maintain in the room was a little bit uncomfortable, but in only his shorts it wasn't bad. The door was locked, so there was no problem of the androids dropping by and he had plenty of cold water in his refrigerator.

"I had better check in with the boys and I had better spruce up a little." This done, he stepped into the hallway and the air had a very strange smell to it. Into the bridge and at the door, he yelled, "Good morning boys, did I miss anything?"

Legs said, "I don't know."

"No fires or anything?"

"Did you hear us yell, *FIRE*?"

"No."

"Then you didn't miss anything."

Ace said, "In "*SUMMER MADNESS*," the actor didn't get wasted, he went to the pen."

Legs added, "He put a hit out on his mouthpiece."

Al replied, "That's what I would have done too. He sold the guy out."

"Did you get your studying done?"

"I wasn't studying, I was reading the History of Mankind; you should try it."

"Why in the hell would we read the History of Mankind?"

Ace added, "I could care less."

"Well, that's gratitude for you, humans designed and built you."

"They did not, an android did."

"Well, I'm not going to argue religion with a couple androids.   Any chatter between Earth and the computer?"

"Yes."

"Ok, what was it?"

"A cosmic radiation alert. Solar flare. F Deck is off limits for passengers. The computer rotated the ship so the aft is in the direction of the sun."

"You don't have any passengers."

Legs replied, "For your benefit, I guess."

"Thanks for warning me."

"You didn't go to F Deck."

Al replied, "I could have."

"Then we would have warned you."

"I'm going to my room; you two give me a headache."

Legs said, "Androids don't get headaches."

Al opened the captain's quarters door and said, "My God, the stink in here is unbelievable. I never noticed it being that bad before." He immediately shut the door and turned on the micron filter exhaust fan in the room. *"I'm almost afraid to take the lid off a tub."*

"I know it is not supposed to look like that. I never read anything about green foamy mold. Hell, it's got a couple days to go yet. I'm going to have to get a gas mask. I could dump it down the toilet, but I might be dumping perfectly good beer. I'm still going to use a gas mask; there should be one under the sink."

With a gas mask on and a hydrometer in hand, he stuck it down through the foam and watched the gauge. *"One percent alcohol, it's getting there. But crap, it has to taste better than it smells. Well, some cheeses do."*

Al lay on his bed with the gas mask on and thought, *"I can't sleep in this damned thing. I'm going to have to sleep in the next room. The boys are going to smell this shit on my clothes and ask questions. I'll go take a shower, different clothes and just stay out of this damned room until the beer is ready."*

Al spent several days with the boys watching the

remainder of the gangster movies and more than once some of the favorites. Al told the two everything he knew about that era in history and they discussed in depth the mentality of the gangsters. At some point in the discussions, Ace said, "I'm going to make a movie. I can make a better one than those."

Al replied, "I suppose you are going to be the main character and Legs and I will be chasing you and missing you?"

"No, James Cagney will be the main gangster."

"How are you going to pull that off?"

"Pull that off of what?"

Al asked, "How in the hell are you going to do it?"

"I downloaded a program off the space port internet. I can cut, copy and edit from these movies we watched and I can use segments and actors from all of them and make one movie. I haven't tried it yet and I think it will be a long involved process, but if it couldn't be done, this program wouldn't exist."

Al said, "Well, that will be something to see; a gangster movie made by an android."

Legs replied, "Androids would have been better gangsters. They sure as hell wouldn't miss ninety percent of the time. That's why they had Tommy guns, so they could hit something once in a while. Most of Chicago's buildings must have had holes all over them."

Al replied, "An android wouldn't have lasted ten minutes in Chicago."

Legs said to Ace, "I want some androids in that damned movie of yours. Put Edward G Robinson in the movie as an android."

Al yelled, "Do you have no shame? Robinson an android? I don't want Robinson whacked in the first ten minutes and if he's an android, he will be."

"Fat chance of that happening. Ok, I'll make that DeWolf actor an android and he can ice Robinson in the first five minutes."

Ace replied, "Ok, you two, I got it. An android gang and a bunch of human gangsters. That's going to be like target practice for the androids."

Al replied, "Make your stupid ass movie, I'm going to bed."

Legs said, "That's another thing. Don't gangsters ever sleep or eat? Maybe they were androids."

"Blow it out your ass, Legs."

Heading back to his room, Al thought, *"I'll be completely crazy by the time I get to Mars. I won't even give a shit if they execute me, I'll probably ask them to make an exception on Mars and do it right away."*

In the hallway he found the gas mask, *"I hope that ventilation system has been working in that mash room. At any rate I had better open the door, jump in and close it quick before the smell gets into the hallway."*

At the captain's quarters, he thought he could get a hint of a smell. He put on his gas mask, opened the door quickly and jumped inside with the door closing behind him. "*My God. I can smell it with the gas mask on.*" The room was hot and moist and Al went to the first tub and took the lid off. "*That is disgusting,*" as he looked at several different colored molds and fungus with small bubbles forming and popping. "*Without this gas mask, I would be a dead man. This can't be right.*" With a kitchen ladle, he pushed it down through the mold and fungus and withdrew some liquid. "*It's about the color of beer, with a green tint to it.*" He ladled a glass full of the liquid that had all kinds of particles floating in it. "*Well, at least none of them are wiggling. Let's see if the mad scientist has made alcohol. I know, I'll call it Frankenbeer. The recipe said it should be about five percent.*"

Looking at the hydrometer, he mumbled in the mask, "Fifteen percent? *This Frankenbeer will knock you on your ass. At the risk of dying an antagonizing death, I have to taste this stuff. I couldn't possibly taste anything in here, I'll take a juice bottle full to the other room. I'll jump in the shower, clothes, gasmask and all and try to wash this stink off.*"

With bottle in hand, he ran to his room next door and jumped in the shower; gas mask and all. Undressing in the shower and letting the gas mask and his clothes fall, he scrubbed down with an aromatic soap and the odor was at a minimum. With the now washed bottle on the table and fresh clothes on, he sat watching the small particles in the beer float around. He unscrewed the lid and before the smell could get to him, he stuck his nose close and sniffed, shook his head and put the lid back on the bottle. *"I don't even have to taste it to know this shit would kill me. Somethings not right. It could be the freeze dried wheat, but it's probably that damned yeast. It was probably yeast for Limburger cheese. Well, shit. So much for the cold beer, and decontamination of that other room is out of the question. The coppers will hang me for this even if I did beat the other rap."*

The bottle of Frankenbeer was flushed down the toilet and the ventilator was on full. He crawled into bed trying to get the lingering smell out of his nostrils and hoping to go to sleep. *"Fifteen percent alcohol, that's something. I wish I had the fifteen percent alcohol out of one of those tubs, I would drink it and pass out."* Not being very sleepy and his mind wandering, he thought, *"What if I could get the fifteen percent of alcohol out of that mess. My God, I'm a moonshiner. They did it out under a walnut tree; I should be able to do it in a space ship. Hell, I bet the longer that stuff sits; the stronger it's going to get. Now, I wish I had a Canadian Club on the rocks. I don't know any more about moonshining than I do about brewing beer. I know I need a still though, they are always talking about a still. Well, it's back to Google, but now I'll have to wait the fifteen minutes transmission time for everything."*

"How's the movie coming, Ace?"

Ace replied, "The damned transmission time is killing me and that first program was a rip off. I'd like to get my hands on the ass hole that developed it, I would strangle him."

Legs said to Al, "You see what I have had to put up with. He's been this way ever since he thought up that nut job idea of making a movie."

"You might help him you know."

"He won't let me, it's his baby."

Al said, "I shouldn't talk, I'm writing a book."

"You're shitting me?"

"Nope, a gangster story. When me and Ace get finished with our projects, you can judge which is best."

Legs asked, "Androids?"

"Nope, just humans."

"What's the plot?"

"A bank heist and a shake down of some gamblers."

"Again? I could write a story better than that."

Al said, "Oh, shit. I'll be working on my book."

"Let's see. Thirty gallons of mash. Yeah, they called it mash and now I can see why. I figure twenty percent alcohol, that's a shit pot full of alcohol. I have to do it in that room to limit the smell. I don't know what the boys will do if they find out. They might contact Earth or at least the ship's computer. Making moonshine has

to be a fire hazard. I've disconnected all of the sensors in that room, unless there's something I don't know about. I'll have to use some hotplates from the mess hall storage room and it's going to get hot as hell in that room. First, I should probably know something about distilling alcohol and the equipment I'll need. Google, here I come and with that damned fifteen minute transmission time, I might as well be writing a book."

After hours on the space port internet, Al thought, *"This is simpler than making Frankenbeer, if you have the equipment. They have what I need in the medical room if I want to make only a spoonful. I have every room on A Deck to find what I can use without the cameras ratting me out."*

Al started his scavenger hunt with a list in his hand and went from room to room on A Deck. He started with the maintenance room and found a lot of tools he would need and then continued on. After several hours and a couple trips to his room, he had what he thought he could use. Not a damned bit of it was on his list, but it should work. There not being a copper pipe on the entire ship that he could shape into a coil, he tore apart s small refrigeration unit and took the radiator. *"There is no reason in the world this radiator won't work. Cold water running over it and I'm home free."* Al couldn't find a large metal pot of any kind that would hold thirty gallons, so he decided to scale down and just run ten gallons of mash. In the mess kitchen there was a large pressure cooker in the ten gallon range and it was a natural for the task at hand.

With a roll of heat resistant plastic hose and clamps, he moved everything to the captain's quarter's door. With gas mask and rubber gloves on, he opened the door and quickly pushed everything into the room.

"*My God, it's worse than before in here. Whatever is floating around in here gets right through this damned gas mask.*"

In three, hot, moist, stinking hours, Al had everything set up to the point he would pour the mash into the pressure cooker. He removed the lid from one of the large tubs and the contents had changed in character. Now it was blue and green mold and the bubbles had gone. "*It must have worked itself out, I guess. More sugar and I bet it would still be working. The bad news is that I can't lift this damned tub. I'm going to have to ladle it out with a pan into the pressure cooker.*"

"*I feel like throwing up,*" as the last of the mash went into the pressure cooker. He twisted the lid to the lock position and thought, "*It's convenient that this pressure cooker has a temperature gauge right in the lid. Two hundred degrees, I have to keep it right there. I'll have to fiddle with the hot plate control knob until I get a handle on this temperature thing, meaning, I'll have to stay in this hell hole. God only knows what is going to come out of that radiator,*" and smiling, he said, "I had better have my knife ready."

With the temperature climbing towards two hundred degrees, he thought, "*I'm going to overshoot it,*" and he backed off on the heat control. The temperature went to one eighty and started to fall off. "*Too much.*" Adjusting the controls a little, the temperature went to one ninety and leveled off. "*A touch more.*"

"*Ah, the sweet spot. Two hundred degrees. Water running over the radiator; nothing to do now but wait for the Canadian Club ship to come in.*"

"*And here it comes,*" as a drop of clear liquid dropped down into a plastic bucket. "*You never taste the first little bit that comes out of the coils. That's what is said. It has water and a bunch of junk in it. Hell, l I'm happy that it's just clear. Surprises the shit outa me.*"

"*Now we're cooking,*" as a small steady stream of clear liquid ran into the bucket. With about an inch in the bucket, Al said out loud, "Zeke, I think we're ready fer a snort." He dipped a small glass into the liquid and said, "Zeke, it's still warm. Ya wanna try it first? Aw come on, don't be scared. Ok, this ought to put some hair on my chest," and Al smelled the liquid and shrugged and then sipped some of it. Al choked and coughed and rubbed his lips, winced in pain and said, "Zeke, either my mouths on fire or we got us some sippin liquor."

Al sat and watched the pail fill and when the little stream of alcohol slowed to a trickle, he shut down the still. *"I had better get this stuff into the next room before it picks up the smell of this room."*

After his decontamination shower, Al sat at the table with the bucket of alcohol in front of him. He scooped a little into a glass and put it to his lips and there was that burn again. *"How are you supposed to drink this shit? I have to cut it with something. I know, what about fruit juice, there's some orange drink powder in the cupboard."*

With a pitcher of imitation flavored orange drink, he filled a water glass and thought, *"I had better write this down. Cup of orange juice and a quarter cup of moonshine and if it isn't strong enough, I can add more moonshine."* Adding ice, he sipped his drink and took another sip and thought, *"Now, that's some good shit. Has a little bite to it, but not bad. I can live with it. How about a good movie and a cold drink,"* and he made his way to his bed, drink in hand and with his back against the wall sipped his drink, *"Boy, I have a hell of a mess in that other room. I'm exhausted from sitting over there in that damned sauna all day."* He finished his cold drink and went to sleep.

When waking, he thought, *"I'm still wasted from being in that damned room next door all day and I have to make a decision. Run the other twenty gallons of mash and then decontaminate that room or just dump the mash and then clean it up."*

Doing the math, at two drinks a day for the

remainder of the trip, he was not going to run short, but what the hell.

"I'll run one more batch and call it quits. I have the still's temperature problem in hand, so I can just start it up and leave the damned thing. I'll start it up, shower and go talk to the boys for a while and come back and shut her down. It'll take a while flushing down the old mash from the first batch. I wonder if the boys are getting suspicious. Anything short of smoke and I should be alright. I've been busy writing a book. Hell, it takes some people forever to write a book."

Al yelled, "This is a stickup, hands in the air, you two," and Legs and Ace didn't even turn around.

Ace said, "The jig's up, Legs. We got cornered by a no good flatfoot."

Legs replied, "Well, he ain't taking me alive."

Al said, "No problem there, you ain't never been alive. How's the movie coming, Ace?"

"I'm working on a scene in the prison lunch room."

"What in the hell would androids be doing in the lunchroom?"

"They are the waiters and they are going to break out of the kitchen."

Al replied, "This ought to be something. No gangster breaks out of a kitchen, they never even go in a kitchen. Could you imagine James Cagney as a waiter in a lunchroom?"

"That's how he fooled them."

"Ok, ok, enough. Don't tell me the story now; it would ruin it for me."

Ace replied, "Ok, smart ass, you can count on me not telling you any more about my movie."

"Legs, how long to Mars?"

"Twenty nine Earth days. The space port sent you all of the way to Mars to open a can of corned beef and hide nine or ten things in your room?"

"That's more than you've done."

"Yeah, but we aren't getting paid."

"They don't pay you?"

Ace said, "Now what would we do with credits? We don't need anything and don't want anything."

Al replied, "That being the case, you wouldn't make much of a gangster. What would be the point?"

"I could win. It was just a human game anyway, wasn't it? Winning and being number one?"

"Now that you mention it, kinda."

Legs said, "I like to win. I play computer games all of the time. If I win I get points and you try to get the most points. All of the players have points. In War of Jupiter, I have 175,000 points. If I bump off three hundred players, I will have the most."

"Well, that's interesting, Legs. Any chatter between the computer and Earth?

"Something about a ship lockdown when in Mars orbit. Probably that deal you have going."

Al said, "I'm not at liberty to say," and he thought, "*Those coppers are playing hardball. No escaping on this trip.*" "Well, you boys keep at it, I don't want to get writers block."

"What's that?"

"When you can't think of what you're going to do next."

Ace said, "Foot, You've had that for some time now."

"Ok, W. C. Fields."

"Who was that?"

"It's a secret, but he would be a natural for your gangster movie. Thinking of him, I have work to do."

At an estimated end distilling time, Al dressed in his detox gear for the distilling room and entered, shut the still down, retrieved the alcohol and then thought, *"I'm going to clean this damned mess up and get it over with."* Many hours passed and Al had everything out of the captain's quarters, but the stink. With a very strong disinfectant, he wiped and sprayed down everything and without the gas mask on he would have choked to death. *"That ought to do it. Now a shower and a cold drink. I have to name this drink."* After giving it some thought in the shower, *"Mickey Finn, that's it. A Mickey Finn on the rocks and I'm going to crash in that bed. I bet I lost twenty pounds in that sauna room."*

He woke at noon Cape Canaveral time, ate a chunk of imitation sausage from the freezer with crackers and thought, *"I wonder what the boys are up to. Better make an appearance at the risk of them driving me nuts."*

"Hello boys, it's me again."

Legs replied, "Imagine that. Who else could it be? We smelled you before you opened the door."

"That bad, huh?"

"Do all humans smell that bad?"

"Yes."

Ace said, "I wondered what those showers were for. The smell mustwash off. You didn't used to smell this bad. You need a shower, I guess."

"Yeah, that's it. I invented a new orange drink; I call it a Mickey Finn."

Ace asked, "It knocks you out like in the movies?"

"No, I just named it that."

Legs said, "Interesting. No, actually it isn't."

Al said, "We are past the point of no return aren't we?"

"If you are asking if we are closer to Mars than Earth, the answer is, yes."

"Done with that academy award winner yet, Ace?"

"Academy award?"

Al said, "Don't worry about it; it was before your time."

"Everything is before my time. My time is one o'clock Cape Canaveral time."

Al said, "I'm out of here, you boys need anything?"

Legs replied, "What in the hell would we be

needing?"

"How about a sense of humor?"

Back in his room and on his bed reading one of the few worn out books lying around, Al thought, "*I feel like a cool one.*" He went through the bartender motions of adding the orange juice and alcohol in a jar, shook it vigorously and then poured it over ice. "*This stuff is smooth as silk,*" as he sipped the drink. An hour later he mixed another drink and thought, "*I thought this stuff would make me sleepy, but it doesn't. I think I'll go see the boys.*"

"Honey, I'm home," as Al made his way onto the bridge.

Ace said, "I'm not changing names."

Legs asked, "What do you want, you were already in here today."

"What's it to ya, big boy? Don't you guys ever lighten up?"

Ace said to Legs, "I think Foot has had a stroke, he is slurring his words."

"I think you're right, what is the procedure?"

"It says, take him to sick bay."

Al said, "Hey, ass holes, I ain't goin ta sick bay."

Ace said, "Maybe he's been poisoned."

"I ain't ate nothin, but a couple Mickey Finns."

Legs replied, "You're pickled."

"On orange juice?"

"If it's just orange juice, you call it orange juice, not Mickey Finn. Did you put a drug in it out of freight?"

"No, absolutely not."

Ace said, "He's drunk. If orange juice sat out, it could ferment."

Legs said, "Ok, Foot. Being drunk is a fire hazard."

"Aw, bullshit, fire hazard. Orange juice ain't no fire hazard. I just need some sleep. I'm going to bed," and Al made his way to the door.

"What a headache. My God. Well, I guess the cats out of the bag and I wonder what those two are going to do? They are going to be in deep shit when we get to Mars and the space port finds I was making alcohol in the captain's quarters. They'll never get the stink out of that place. I had better get with them and come up with a story that gets them off the hook. They had nothing to do with it. The only way out for them is if they contact Mars now and tell them they just discovered what I was doing. No difference to me, I'm going to get whacked anyway. I had better hide one of these jugs of alcohol in case the androids confiscate it. Might as well stay drunk for a month. Well, let's do it, Cagney."

CHAPTER THREE

NEUTRAL SPACE

 Al entered the bridge without one of his greetings and went to the monitor next to Legs and Ace.

Legs said, "We did a little checking with the Quality Control Department at Cape Canaveral Space Port."

"And?"

"It's on the monitor."

Alphonse Bruni
Age 35
Space Corp Sergeant
Awaiting trial for homicide and drug trafficking

Fugitive presently at large and on the Space Freighter 2772

Trial will be held in Tampa Florida on Bruni's return from Mars.

"Well boys, that's the way the cookie crumbles."

Legs asked, "Is that some kind of analogy of this situation. A crumbling cookie?"

"How about, it is what it is?"

"You could say that about anything, besides homicide and drug trafficking."

Ace said, "Foot, who did you rub out?"

"I didn't rub him out, one of his drugged up customers did."

"What happened to the customer?"

"He got two weeks in detox."

"And you get arrested for homicide?"

"The shits, isn't it. That's a death sentence."

Legs asked, "Death sentence?"

"Yeah, homicide."

"That is the shits."

"Can't you get a mouthpiece?"

"Oh yeah. A Corp lawyer."

Ace said, "That's no good. The Corp probably isn't too happy about one of their own being a bad egg."

"Yeah, and that trip back to Earth isn't going to be a Disneyworld ride."

"Disneyworld?"

"Forget it. Mars to Earth will be my last space

flight."

Legs said, "Ours too."

"Why's that?"

"Being replaced with the new ZZZ 223234 models."

"Well, that's the shits, too. Then what will you do?"

"We will be recycled for component parts."

Al said, "Recycled. That doesn't sound like much fun either."

Legs replied, "I don't know."

"Well, they are putting the screws to all of us then."

"That's the schedule."

"I was worried I might have caused you some trouble making moonshine."

Ace said, "Making moonshine?"

"Yeah, in the captain's quarters."

"Like in, *SOUTHERN TROUBLE?*"

"Kinda like that, yeah."

"Will you show me some moonshine? It's in my movie."

"Sure, I'll show you some. Sorry about coming in here shitfaced yesterday."

Legs replied, "That's ok, we get that way sometimes if one of our batteries is low."

Ace asked, "Can we go now?"

Al replied, "Let's do it, but I don't want to hear a bunch of bullshit about fire hazards."

Al took the two to his room and showed them about five gallons of white lightning in jars in his refrigerator.

Ace asked, "Foot, how much does it take to get pickled?"

"Obviously, about a half a cup,"

"Mixed in orange juice?"

Al replied, "Yes."

"I need to change that in my movie. The bar is mixing it with water."

"Water?"

"Yes."

"That's criminal."

Legs asked, "Where is the still?"

"It's in the closet in the captain's quarters. You don't want to go in there."

"Yes, I do."

"Fine," and he led the two to the captain's quarters, opened the door and said, "After you."

"What is that smell? It's terrible."

"Fermented mash. I distilled the alcohol out of it."

"Does the alcohol taste like that?"

"No, do you want to taste it?"

Legs replied, "Now why would I be able to taste anything?"

"Well, sorry. You can smell."

"Yes, anything burning or any smell due to a fire. We don't go around licking things to see if there is a fire."

"What a smart ass. The still is in the closet."

Ace opened the closet door and said, "That will work?"

Al replied, "Of course it will work, it did work. That alcohol sells for about two thousand credits a quart on Mars."

Legs replied, "My guess is, you aren't going to have time to sell it."

"That's why I'm going to drink it all before we get there."

"You do that, but just stay off the bridge. And carry a fire extinguisher with you at all times. That stuff is highly flammable."

"I think I'll have me a Mickey Finn right now. Join me? We can yank a couple of your batteries."

"No, thank you."

"In that case, I'll see you boys tomorrow."

Many hours later and with a hangover, Al entered the bridge and the androids watched him closely. Al thought, *"They must not be horsing around about me being drunk in here,"* and he said, "I'm sober as a judge."

Legs replied, "Good."

"I was just wondering, Legs, "Why didn't they send one of those little fast ships and just take me off of this one? They wouldn't have to wait a month to nab me."

"I can only assume that they would have been too late in pursuit."

Al said, "Hell, it wasn't that long until they figured out I was on this ship. They could have caught up to us in a couple weeks."

"Yes, and that was too late. We would be in the neutral space."

"What in the hell is neutral space? I never heard of it."

"Not many people have because it has never mattered. It was adopted and agreed upon a hundred years ago."

Al replied, "Ok, ok, what about us, a faster ship and this neutral space?"

Legs replied, "After one million miles from the Earth, Moon or Mars, a ship enters neutral space. The reason they did not come after the ship is that we would be in neutral space. In neutral space, the authorities, whoever they may be, are out of their jurisdiction."

"You mean to tell me, there is no law out here?"

"Oh, there is normally law. When entering neutral space, the captain of the ship is the authority and the law. In our case, there is no captain of the ship. It was never an issue because androids never break the law."

Al said, "Well, it makes sense. Sort of like old Blackbeard days, huh? The captain is the law."

Legs asked, "Why would beards have anything to do with it?"

"I'm going to go have a Mickey Finn and watch a movie."

Ace replied, "We're going to watch, *SUMMER HEAT* again."

"Good movie; bootlegging bonded scotch."

Before long, Al was back and said, "I'm on the wagon for two days." Having a seat, he asked, "How big is this freighter?"

Ace answered, "Six hundred and forty feet in length and eighty feet in diameter."

"Anti-gravity and nuclear powered, huh?"

"Yes."

"How much freight on board?"

Legs asked, "What is this, a third degree?"

"Just curious."

Ace continued, "Nine hundred and twenty six tons, seventy five pounds."

"That's quite a load. I'll see you boys later, I need a shower."

Legs said, "We had to change our uniforms and wipe down with a cleaning agent to get rid of that smell."

Twelve hours later, it flashed on Ace's monitor, *"Could you boys meet me in my quarters in five minutes?"*

Legs said to Ace, "Maybe he is pickled and can't walk. We had better go see what the problem is," and the two rose and headed for Al's quarters.

"Come in boys and have a seat."

Legs replied, "Ok, spill the beans."

Al said, "There may be some prying eyes on that bridge."

Ace asked, "Are you shitfaced again?"

"*No*, I'm not shitfaced *again*. Just want to have a little heart to heart."

"That doesn't sound like any fun either."

"I just want to discuss our problem."

Legs said, "Our problem?"

"Yes, our problem. What do we three have in common?"

"We are on this space freighter, that's it."

"Yes, but in the future?"

Ace replied, "We are going to get rubbed out on Earth in three months?"

"Exactly. Now what would be a better scenario than that?"

"We don't get rubbed out on Earth in three months?"

"Right again, Ace. You're smarter than you look. Help Legs out if he gets confused."

Legs replied, "I'm confused right now. So what? Is there a point here?"

"Again, here is the final test for you boys. Which scenario would you prefer, getting rubbed out in three months or not getting rubbed out in three months?"

Ace replied, "Foot, we have never considered another scenario where we wouldn't be terminated. But for me, termination seems a bit pointless."

Al said, "How about you, Legs?"

"I'm listening."

"Well, I need some help on this. What could we three do to prevent being rubbed out in three months?

You boys think it over; I'm going to mix a drink."

Al, back with his Mickey Finn in hand, Legs said, "We never get to Mars with the ship."

"Good thinking Legs, could you expand on that?"

"How do you expand on that?"

"What scenario is there where we don't get to Mars?"

"We continue into space or we park the freighter in neutral space."

Al said, "That parking sounds interesting, can we do it?"

"Yes, with some difficulty, but it is possible. Normally a parked ship is in orbit around a planet. It has been done before, to transfer cargo to another ship."

"You are sure about the neutral space thing?"

"Yes."

"Ace, you are the movie maker, how do you see this all playing out?"

"The space port and Earth will want their ship back. There is no law in space, so they will hijack this space ship; or if damaged, offload the cargo."

"How would we prevent that?"

Ace replied, "Tell them we will decompress the cargo hold if they attempt a hijacking."

"What will that do?"

Legs replied, "All of the freight in cans and containers will explode and the fifty tons of wheat will explode."

"Like puffed wheat?"

"What in the hell is puffed wheat?"

"Never mind. So they would lose the cargo?"

"And the ship. Component parts in the reactor engines would be damaged beyond repair. A few freighters have decompressed and they just ejected them into space."

Back to you Ace, "If they lost their ship and cargo anyway, why not just let it be destroyed and sling us into space?"

"We have an open ended negotiation for the return of the ship and cargo. We bullshit them."

"I'm going to like your movie, Ace. Well, what do you think boys? Watch and make movies for twenty years, or the scrap heap?"

Legs replied, "We're going to give the matter some thought. It's not like mugging some drunk in an alley."

"Well, look at it this way. If we can hole up for anything over three months, we are ahead of the game."

"Yeah, if we can. We will do an analysis on the subject and make a determination. But remember this. We are not going to hole up with a booze crazy drunk."

"One Mickey Finn a day, tops."

Al thought, "*I don't want to be too pushy, but it's been a couple days and I haven't heard a peep out of those two. What in the hell is the problem? They'll be made into coat hangers if they don't go along with the deal. No, I had better hang tough. The more they are involved the better. I'll agree with any ideas they have until they are in this up to their asses."*

There was a knock on Al's door and he hid his drink under his bed and yelled, "I wonder who that could be?"

The door opened and Legs and Ace walked in and took a seat at the table along with a pile of papers that they lay on the desk.

Al said, "I was beginning to wonder about you boys."

Legs replied, "Flying this spaceship isn't like driving a Model T Ford you know."

"You are going to park it then?"

"We are going to try to park it."

"You're in on the deal then?"

"What do we have to lose?"

Al asked, "So what's the problem with the ship, you said you could park it."

Ace replied, "The problem is, we don't know how the ships computer is going to react. We fly the ship when the computer doesn't. We aren't sure we can override it."

Al said, "Then we have to get the computer out of the loop."

"That is what these papers are. We couldn't use the computer, so we had to do the calculations by hand."

"So what did you come up with?"

Once the ship is stopped in space, we can override

the computer, so we have to have the computer stop the ship. There are only two scenarios where the ship stops in space and not just the altering of its course."

"And what are they?"

Legs replied, "Biological hazard contamination or an unalterable collision with the Earth, Moon or Mars."

"Couldn't we just short circuit the damned computer?"

"No, and the computer operates the controls until the ship is at full stop, which is normally at a space port. Again, we cannot control the ship until it is at a dead stop and the computer signs off. At that point we hit the control button, *Reprogram*, and it is out of the loop and can't get back in."

Al asked, "Well, what's it going to be. A biological hazard or an uncontrollable ship going to crash into Mars?"

"I just explained the ships controls to you and the computer knows it has control of the ship and will divert it to miss Mars, so it's a biological hazard. At this point, the best chance for that working is if you brought the hazard on board with you in an attempt to punish the Corp on Mars."

Al replied, "You should be making the movie, not Ace. But, what do I have to lose? What do *we* have to lose?"

Legs said, "There is a condition you have to agree to."

"And what's that?"

"If this scheme goes south on us, you deactivate us as if we had no part in it. We have no desire to give androids a bad name. If we do get away with it, we will be android heroes."

"How do I deactivate you two?"

"A switch behind the right ear, and leave a fingerprint."

"BIOHAZARD, BIOHAZARD," flashed on all of the monitors and many places throughout the ship. Within a microsecond the ship started switching end for end and the reactor rockets energized to slow and stop the big space freighter. With an eye on a changing digital number and several gauges, Legs slammed his two hands down on two red buttons and yelled, "She's ours."

Al said, "No shit?"

Legs answered, "We're dead in the water, as Bogart said in, *"TYPHOON."* The ship's computer is lights out, waiting to be reprogrammed."

"That calls for a drink."

Legs said, "Three drinks and we are heading for Earth and some cement boots for you."

Al replied, "What do we do now?"

"Hell, I don't know. What's the other part of your plan?"

"What other part. This was the whole plan."

Ace said, "This could get boring. We have been here five minutes and I'm bored already. I used to never get bored."

Legs replied, "The good news is that now we can get on the interplanetary internet. The computer had us blocked before and limited us to space port internet."

"Why was that?"

"The human crews abused it. Probably skin flicks would be my guess."

Al replied, "We can get skin flicks?"

Ace said, "What do you mean *we*? The most disgusting behavior I have ever witnessed."

"Well, now that you mention it. But, how about old gangster movies?"

Legs replied, "How in the hell would I know? I never heard of them until we got this walking, talking ancient history book on board."

Al asked, "What do you think the space ports are thinking about now?"

"I would assume a spaceship with a biohazard onboard. We had better send a message to them before they send ships out here."

Al replied, "Ok, let's have one Mickey Finn to celebrate. One for each of us."

Legs said, "Ace, get the cuffs."

"Earth, Mars and the Moon space ports

The space freighter2772 has been hijacked by Alphonse Bruni and is parked in neutral space. Alphonse Bruni will negotiate for the exchange of freighter 2272 in exchange for full immunity for any crimes committed in the past, the two androids on board the freighter and transport to Earth. The androids have presently been incapacitated and reprogrammed. The minimum time allowed for these negotiations to be the two years that the freighter will be parked. The ship and cargo will be maintained during that time.

Any attempt to board or manipulate the freighter will result in the freight decks being decompressed, resulting in a total loss of the freight and the ship. Any space ship on an intersecting course and within one thousand miles will be considered a hijacking with the resulting damage.

Have a nice day. Alphonse Bruni"

Al said to his fellow hijackers, "Well, that ought to do it; we'll see what they say."

Ace asked, "Have a nice day? How could they have a nice day?"

"It wouldn't be easy under the circumstances. It's not going to be any picnic here either."

"Picnic?"

"Whatever. Let's try that interplanetary internet, you boys might learn something. I bet there are all kinds of good movies on it."

Legs replied, "Fine, we'll take turns selecting them."

"Fair is fair."

"Ace and I have decided to rename you."

Al said, "I was beginning to like, Foot."

"We're going to call you, *Boss* until you drink three Mickey Finns in twenty four hours and then we are going to call you Ass Hole from then on."

"Well, Ass Hole has kind of a nice ring to it, but I can live with Boss."

There was an immediate reply demanding the freighter continue on to Mars, but it failed to mention any consequences if it didn't. A military ship was in route to the location of the freighter and again consequences were not mentioned.

Al said, "Well, it'll be a month before anything gets here if they leave right away. There may be other freighter ships and passenger ships passing by and they may not know about us, so we had better not get trigger happy."

Ace said, "Trigger happy?"

Al said, "I thought you could speak English?"

"I can, it's you that's having the problem."

Al replied, "Let's send another message reaffirming our position on this matter. After their threats, there will be the negotiations. We can reply to that after we see what they say. Meanwhile, Legs, fire up that internet."

On the bridge, the internet was on three monitors as the three watched what was happening on Earth, the Moon and Mars.

Ace yelled, "Hey, we're in the news. A space port

freighter was hijacked. The other two looked at Aces monitor at a news caster telling the unbelievable story about a Corp sergeant hijacking a space freighter. The original message they had sent was displayed on the monitor and then four people at a table were discussing the hijacking and how it was even possible.

Al said, "Top of the world, Ma."

"Yeah, but I hope we don't get burned alive like Cagney did."

Al replied, "Using the term **alive**, loosely in your case. I know my first movie pick."

Ace asked, "What's that?"

"Pinocchio."

Legs said, "Sounds like an Italian gangster movie."

"Sort of."

"Well, let's watch it, we aren't learning anything on the news we don't already know."

Al said, "My room, on the big screen."

Al made himself a Mickey Finn and the three sat and Al searched and found the movie Pinocchio and started it on the big screen.

Ace asked, "Is this one of those cartoons? The people don't look real."

"Pretend it's an android movie."

Nothing else was said during the movie and after the credits, Legs asked, "Who in the hell would want to be a human?"

Ace replied, "Not me."

Al replied, "Me either. I'm tired of waking up every three hours to take a piss."

"That wouldn't bother me much, I'm already up."

Legs said, "Seriously, I enjoyed that movie much more than the gangster movies."

Ace replied, "Not me. Pinocchio was sort of a gangster though. Boss, what do you think?"

Al replied, "He reminds me of me."

Legs added, "He reminds me of you too. But in your case, lying without the nose job."

"Alright boys, enough fun for one night. I'm going to get on one of my movie blogs and talk to a human."

"Well, that doesn't sound like much fun to me."

"There's a bunch of dudes out there that are old movie nuts.

Legs replied, "I'm not even going to ask what all that means."

"Good. You two find us a movie to watch."

With the two now out of his room, Al logged on to his old "Flicker" blog with his normal blog handle being "Blackjack." He chatted back and forth with several of his old bloggers who wondered what had happened to him because he had been absent for months. He made no mention of his situation with the space ship and there was no reason for them to connect Blackjack with Alphonse Bruni or a space ship. It was for the most part just old movie talk between people on the Earth, Moon and Mars.

The next message from the Mars Space Port was as to be expected; that if he turned himself in, his case would be reviewed and given further consideration.

Legs asked, "Boss, you buying that crap?"

"Was I born yesterday?"

"What kind of a question was that?"

"That was a, *No, I'm not buying that crap question.* We'll just string them along with; we don't trust them and so on. I'll tell them I am playing hardball with them and contact me a year from now. That's a year I know I am going to be alive."

Ace said, "Hardball? How is playing a game going to help?"

The three spent their days watching movies and trolling the internet and frequently the parked space freighter was mentioned on the internet, but there were no details to speak of. Al communicated with his "Flicker," group and for the most part everything was going fine with an occasional message from the space ports with more proposals.

Ace said, "Look,Boss, that's you on the internet," as his Corp I.D. was shown and some details of his life. His infatuation with historic gangsters and movies was also mentioned and that this may have led to Al's criminal behavior.

A month passed and the three continued to keep

themselves occupied with the internet movies and Al on his blog site talking to real humans. Numerous messages had been received from the space ports with all kinds of suggestions that would be good for Al.

Ace said to Al, "They tried to hack the ship's computer, but we had anticipated that. It's dead as a door knob."

"Good work boys, I'm not real good with computers."

"You can say that again. No, don't say it again."

"What?"

Legs said, "You know what? And you are a cup of alcohol short in one of the jugs. What did you do, spill some?"

"That's it, I spilled some."

"Well, be careful about the spillage. Ten years locked in a broom closet could get real boring."

Al replied, "I'll tell you what wouldn't get boring. A couple welding leads up your ass."

Legs replied, "Tonight, we are going to watch, *PLANET OF THE APES.*"

"What in the world is an ape?"

"I thought you would know."

"Why would I know. A planet somewhere with apes? There aren't any planets with apes, whatever they are."

Ace said, "I think they are androids."

Al replied, "One more reason it isn't going to be worth a shit. But, a deal's a deal."

When the movie was over, Al said, "Nice pick, Legs. Where did you find that in the worst ten movies section?"

"Well, it didn't surprise me that the monkeys were smarter than the humans. What the hell was that movie about?"

"I have no idea. I'll ask one of my blogger friends."

Blackjack: *"Hood, you online?"*
Hood: *"Go ahead Blackjack."*
Blackjack: *"Have you watched, Planet of the Apes?"*
Hood: *"No, is it any good?"*
Blackjack: *"No, about a bunch of monkeys."*
Hood: *"Why did you watch that?"*
Blackjack: *"It's a long story. Are you still into those detective movies?"*
Hood: *"Yes, but I mix it up. I have a question for you Blackjack."*
Blackjack: *"Shoot."*
Hood; *"Are you A.B.?"*
There was a long pause and Al answered back, *Blackjack*: *"AB positive."*
Hood: *"It adds up. Do you have a secure email?"*
Blackjack: *"I will have. I'll get it to you tomorrow."*
Hood: *"Roger."*
Blackjack: *Out."*

Al thought, *"I don't know if this is a good thing or not. Hood nailed me. Maybe I can get some inside dope on what the space ports are doing about us out here. Can't hurt."*

With the help of Ace and Legs, Al set up an encrypted email and got the email address to Hood by telling him the email address was the first two words in Hood's favorite book. Hood set up another email address and the two were good to go on encrypted emails.

Hood wrote, *"Good show Blackjack. I laughed my ass off when you told me you were AB. How in the hell did you pull off a caper like that? I am on Mars and like everyone else I revolve in and out every two years. Damned Planetary Service. I'll be twenty six next year, so I'll be out of this mandatory service crap. I'm kind of a stuck in the mud, so not much to say other than movies. Email me how you ended up out there in that parked freighter. Not too much on TV about it.*
Hood."

Al replied with a long email pretty well telling Hood the whole story of how he got there and what it has been like on the freighter."

The immediate reply was, *"You have alcohol? You made alcohol on that ship?"*

Al replied, *"A few gallons."*

Hood replied, *"You know what that would be worth on Mars? There isn't a drop of alcohol on Mars and not a drop gets here from Earth. Twenty years in the pen for possession."*

And so the emails went back and forth for weeks between Al and Hood and out of the blue, Hood asked if it would be alright if he and a crew of twenty stopped at the freighter on their way to Earth. They would be on one of the small fast galaxy passenger ships. It was a private carrier space craft and he had already discussed it with everyone. The incentive was the alcohol they could get from Al. Maybe party on the freighter and then a supply for the month trip to Earth from there.

Legs said, "Maybe it's a trap by the space ports."

Al replied, "I don't think so. What could they do anyway if it was a trap? You and Ace will be locked in on A Deck, so no one can get to the bridge. That, and you can decompress the lower decks and wipe them out. It won't hurt to have some friends on Earth and Mars, you guys might need a spare part sometime. Those damned batteries of yours won't last forever, rechargeable or not."

Ace said, "I don't see what it would hurt. Some different humans on board would be refreshing. I want to see if they are all like ours."

Al replied, "Ours? Oh, the shoe is on the other foot now, huh?"

Legs said, "This is a Democracy. One man one vote."

"You're right. One *Man* one vote."

Ace said, "Bullshit."

Al said, "I'll tell Hood that it's ok, but to keep it under his hat."

Legs said to Ace, "How does he keep coming up with this bullshit gibberish? Under his hat?"

"It means, keep it quiet."

"It still doesn't make any sense; under his hat."

"It means, to keep it in his brain."

"Why not just say that then?"

"Did you get the wheat, Ace?"

"Yeah, I got into the seed being sent to Mars."

"Well, we'll have to cut back on the water then. It won't sop up water like that freeze dried stuff. Legs, do you think four runs will be enough?"

"I'm going to say, yes, so we won't be doing five."

Al replied, "Oh, yeah, take all the fun out of it."

"Fun? If I knew what fun was, I would probably think this is not fun."

"Ok. Four tubs of mash all working at the same time for about two weeks, maybe three, and then two days cooking it off. We'll be done long before Hood and his bunch get here."

Legs said, "I hope the captain of that ship knows how to dock with this freighter. We don't need a big hole in the side of it."

"No sweat."

Legs said, "Ace, did you hear that? No sweat."

"I heard."

With four tubs of mash mixed and covered, Ace said, "It doesn't smell at all"

Al replied, "Give it a chance."

"Does it look different after it ferments?"

"No, just the same. In a week or so you can come check it."

"Why would I check it if it is going to be just the same?"

"Just in case."

"In case of what?"

"I don't know, a fire or something."

Legs said, "I installed surveillance cameras and a carbon detector, so we could see a fire."

Al said, "My God, how hard is it to lift the lid on a tub. We might have to add more water or something."

Ace replied, "Ok, ok, I'll be the the mash checker."

Al said to Legs, "It's your movie pick tonight unless you want to let me do it."

"No thanks. Tonight we're watching *"NIGHT OF THE ZOMBIES."* I think it's about a bunch of New York City Italians. I saw the previews."

"You do all of this to just piss me off, don't you, Legs?"

"A deal is a deal."

Al said, "You didn't think I could sit through that whole zombie movie did you, Legs?"

Ace asked, "Were those guys that were killing zombies, Mafia?"

"No, they were all android design engineers yelling, this was a bad idea."

"Should I check the mash now?"

"Yeah. Once now and then again next week."

Ace left and returned and said, "You were right AL, it looks just the same."

Al replied, "I told you."

The week passed slowly and there was a faint smell coming from the sealed captain's quarters and it was the same smell as the three had encountered during Al's first run of alcohol.

The three when sitting on the bridge, Ace said, "I'm going to go check the mash now."

Al replied, "Ok."

A few minutes later on the computer monitors in red, flashed, BIOHAZARD, BIOHAZARD and Al and Legs looked at the surveillance camera monitors where Ace was yelling, "Should I leave the door sealed?"

With red lights flashing, Al broke into laughter and Legs looked at him like he was crazy and said, "What's the deal?"

"Everything's ok, it just looks and smells like there's a biohazard onboard, it just means the mash is right on schedule." Al then yelled into the microphone, "It's ok Ace, wipe down, change clothes and come on back. And turn those damned alarms off."

Ace yelled back, "You ass hole."

When Ace returned in a clean uniform, Al said, "I thought you were going to wipe down?"

"I did, ass hole."

"Maybe you should try some tomato juice, it works on skunks."

"I don't know what either of those are, but I'll be getting even with you."

"Seriously, what did it look like?"

"Seriously? Well, seriously, I think it would kill a human."

Al replied, "It probably would, but we are distilling the alcohol out of it."

Ace replied, "I can't even imagine what it will look like in another week."

"You should have worn the gas mask."

"I don't inhale, I just smell."

"Well, no harm done."

Ace replied, "You are now the official mash checker, I did my time."

"Ok, ok. In seven days we'll start distilling."

Legs replied, "What do you mean *we*. Those aren't my drunken buddies dropping by for a party."

Ace asked, "What are we getting out of this?"

"The experience. How many androids can say they ran four batches of moonshine? Your friends hear about it and they'll be jealous as hell."

"We don't have any friends."

"Well, you probably will after this caper. Anyway, I'm getting tired of wearing these damned uniforms, how about you boys?"

Legs replied, "We always wore uniforms."

Ace said, "That's all there is on the ship. For the crews."

"How about in freight?"

"Garments?"

"Yeah, I guess."

"There are garments."

Al said, "Well, let's check it out."

Legs said, "I want a suit like Humphrey Bogart wears."

"Ok, let's go shopping."

Al said, "You didn't tell me this was in freight. Hazmat suits."

Legs replied, "We didn't tell you about the baby carriages either."

"We can use one of these."

"There you go with that *we* again."

"Well, let's snag a couple of these and get to the garments. Boxes 111, 112, 113, 114."

After a huge mess was made on E Deck with clothes scattered everywhere, the three were all dressed in outfits as characteristic as they could get to what a modern day gangster would wear. The three became somewhat overdressed as it had turned into an outlandish attire competition.

Al said, "You two could use a little makeup, you both look like a couple cheap wrist watches in suits."

Ace said, "Well, it wasn't androids that invented makeup, it was humans."

Al replied, "Once in a while there is an ugly one."

Legs said to Ace, "Just our luck."

Ace replied, "I feel kind of naked not packing some iron."

Al said, "Well, that changing clothes answered that question."

Legs replied, "What question was that?"

"The answer is, you two would be shit out of luck if you had to take a piss."

"It's all about skin flicks with you isn't it. I'm not sure just exactly how that thing works, would you explain it to us?"

Al said, "I know what my next movie pick is going to   be."

Ace replied, "Ohhhh nooo."

"Fair is fair. I'm going to grab some food from F Deck. I'm about out. I'll see you two on the bridge."

When Al arrived at the bridge, Ace said, "You got mail."

On the monitors was a letter from Mars Space Port wanting to know the status of the ship and there was a list of requested details."

Legs said, "They want to make sure the freight is being maintained. They want a read out of the condition of the ship and its contents."

"Makes sense. I think they're getting an itchy

trigger finger. You boys handle that, I'm going to try out one of the hazmat suits and check the mash. It's my turn, Ace. And don't forget it's movie night."

"Let's run the still, boys. You can tell by the smell of the mash that it's going to be quality liquor."

Legs replied, "Ok, we'll help, just for the experience."

Al said, "You know, it isn't just everybody that has a moonshine still on a rocket ship."

"No, I didn't know that."

Ace asked, "How many jugs ya figure, Rusty?"

Al replied, "Bout sixteen a figure, Zeke. And first class sippin liquor, too."

"Take yer head right off, I'm bettin."

Legs said, "Enough. Let's get it over with. The only thing I can think of that I would rather not do is sit through another one of those disgusting skin flicks."

Al replied, "There are better ones than that one was."

"I doubt that."

In biohazard suits, the three got the first batch on the burner and retired to Al's room where they played some stupid video game just to humor Ace. This game evolved into gambling between the three and what they gambled for were their turns at movie selections and the least desirable jobs in the distilling process. After weeks of playing this gambling video game, Legs had won five movie picks each from the other two and they were desperate to get them back from Legs. The desperation was caused by Leg's last picks of *"SPACE BUCCANEERS"* and *"STAGE COACH."*

An email came through from Hood that their ship would rendezvous with the freighter in two days and the docking procedure was not a problem. The captain of the ship was an old Corp freighter captain that went private. Their ship has been cloaked for two days, to maintain radio silence. "This little stop is off the books. Savvy?"

CHAPTER FOUR

VISITORS

Legs said, "They're docking at F Deck docking port."

Al said, "We'll let them board and have a little heart to heart before I go down there. The gravity is at point eight?"

"Yes, point eight."

The smaller passenger ship successfully docked with the freighter and eventually twenty three people were on F Deck walking around in the freight. At a reconnaissance camera, Hood said, "AB, you there?"

"Yes, I'm here Hood. How sure are you about that bunch with you?"

"One hundred percent."

Al replied, "Ok. My android friends are prepared to decompress decks C, D, E and F if there is any attempt to take over the ship."

Hood replied, "No sweat."

"Come on up to C Deck, the cafeteria there."

"On our way."

As Al waited for his guests, it sounded like a parade coming his way with all the chatter and yelling and laughing. A long line of men entered the cafeteria and in the lead was who must be Hood. He walked directly to Al and shook his hand and said, "This is really something. I just met my first hijacker."

"Well, it's not all it's cracked up to be," replied Al.

Hood turned and yelled to his companions, "Have a seat, you jerks." He waved to an older gentleman in a uniform and he came and joined Hood and Al.

"Al, this is Captain Accardi, like yourself, an Italian New Yorker."

Further introductions followed and Hood was identified as Sergeant Sanduski, also a New Yorker.

Captain Accardi said to Al, "I hope you have some liquor or there could be a lynching at hand."

Al replied, "In the fridge and you had better like orange juice."

"If it's got alcohol in it, I could drink rat piss."

Al said to the bunch, "There are coffee cups in the cupboard, help yourself, we'll get the booze."

Hood said, "Speakeasy style. Well, that's certainly appropriate."

Al had premixed the alcohol and the orange drink and he, the Captain and Hood brought bottle after bottle to the tables. It could be overheard that the crowd was liking the drink and there were some saying, "This shit is pretty good."

Al said to Hood and the Captain, "Come into my office," and the three with a couple bottles retired to a small adjacent room.

The Captain said, "Made this booze right here on this ship, huh?"

"That we did."

The Captain frowned and said, "We? How many people know we stopped here?"

"Just me."

"Then who are *we*?"

Al replied, "My two android partners."

"The androids are your partners? They are space port property."

"Not any more, they aren't."

"Well, I guess stranded with two robots is better than with no one. Do they do what you tell them?"

"You don't tell those two to do anything. You ask them and usually they tell you to stick it in your ass."

"The robots?"

Al said, "Androids. And I wouldn't say robots

around them."

The Captain said, "It sounds to me like they are a little pushy for androids. Must be a new model. All of them I ever saw just sat and looked at a computer monitor."

Al said, "Hood, what do you think of the booze?"

"My god, how strong is this stuff? I'm getting cross eyed already."

"Three tall drinks and you're on your ass."

"I can believe that. It's getting a little loud out there in the cafeteria."

Al said, "How about some roaring twenties music?"

Hood replied, "I'm up for it, but that bunch out there won't have a clue."

"It sounds like it won't make any difference. Legs, put on some Jazz."

From the PA system came a reply, "Ok, Boss."

Hood said, "Boss? I like it."

Jazz began playing and the Captain said, "I hope those two don't take offense to what I was saying."

Al replied, "They allow for misconduct by humans. It's our nature. Probably the New York in us."

"So they just operate the controls on the ship?"

"Hell, one of them is writing a book and the other is making a gangster movie."

The Captain said, "You're shitting me? And they are watching us all the time?"

"Part of the deal. They are ready to decompress the ship."

Hood said, "Decompress the ship?"

"Our safety protocol if a ship hijacking attempt takes place."

"Well, I might be a Nervous Nellie, but assure them that's not going to happen."

Al said, "I can only have two Mickey Finns a day. I named this drink, Mickey Finn."

"And what if you violate the rules?"

Al replied, "They mentioned ten years in a broom closet."

The captain said, "Sounds like they are running the show."

"Nope. Three way deal. Partners."

"Interesting. Well, I can tell that by the time this bunch quenches their thirst, they are going to be lying all over that cafeteria."

On the speaker, Ace said, "Get them into the rooms before they pass out and they can clean up the puke in the morning."

The Captain replied, "Aye, aye sir. Well, house rules; let's get with it."

The speaker said, "Tonight we are broadcasting, *SNOW WHITE AND THE SEVEN DWARFS.*"

The Captain said, "Snow White and the Seven Dwarfs?"

"Ace is just joking."

Laughing, Hood said, "Ace?"

The Captain asked, "And the other?"

"Legs."

"Those two drink this stuff."

Al replied, "No. Too smart and no stomach."

Hood asked, "You're sure there is not a decompression problem?"

"One hundred percent."

"Well then, me and the Captain are going to our rooms and get plastered. Tell that Ace machine that he can go ahead and put on Snow White and the Seven Dwarfs. It's a cocaine thing isn't it?"

"Yeah, sort of."

Ace said to Al, "I'm not sure this is such a good idea. They tore that cafeteria up. How long are they going to stay?"

"Well, you can figure tomorrow for sure, with the hangovers and all."

Legs said, "They're on their own. There are housemaid androids, but I'm not one of them."

"Settle down, Legs. They'll be out of here soon enough."

"Not soon enough for me."

Al replied, "You might want to have some android friends stop in some day and I'm going to be just as bitchy as you are."

"Bitchy?"

"Yeah, like pissing and moaning."

"Oh, like pissing and moaning; whatever that means."

"Anything from Mars?"

"Nothing. I think we wore them down. They hear about this little shindig we have going here and it'll be a different story."

"Well, they aren't going to hear, are they?"

"Not unless one of them troops runs off at the mouth. My God, I can't even speak English anymore."

Al replied, "Sounds like perfect English to me."

"Well it isn't; and you think I'm bad, Ace has been watching some old Oklahoma movies."

"*GRAPES OF WRATH?*"

"One of them."

"Where is he?"

"Faulty thermal detector on B deck."

"I only had one Mickey Finn for medicinal purposes and I'm going to my room and get some sleep. Wake me at seven."

"Have to keep throwing in the little android digs don't you. Now I'm an alarm clock. It's called being prejudice."

"Prejudice against androids?"

"Hell, yes, all humans are."

"I hadn't thought about it, I suppose you're right."

At seven, Al woke to Ace yelling over his room PA, "The early bird gets the worm."

Al replied, "I suggest you lay off the movies for a while."

He made his way to the bridge and Legs said, "Well, they are up and at it again. You know what they are doing now?"

"I couldn't even guess."

"Mixing alcohol, water and freeze dried tomato paste."

Al replied, "That might work. I think they called them Bloody Harrys."

"It's not working for me. We already had a smoke alarm go off. One of them frying dried eggs I think. There are some dried eggs missing from F Deck."

"I'll take care of it. Maybe I can hurry them out of here. Although talking to a human was nice, considering."

Legs said, "Considering, what?"

"Considering I've been teaching school for months."

"Yeah, and when you peak out at the sixth grade, we'll take over."

"Kind of touchy this morning, aren't we?"

"That's to be expected, considering."

Al said, "Ok, ok. I'm going below. You're kind of quiet Ace. Now what's *your* problem."

"I'll watch movies if I want to."

"Fine."

When Al got to the cafeteria down below, it was buzzing with conversation and almost all of it was about the party last night and how drunk everyone got. There were the Blood Harrys being carried around and the Captain and Hood were circulating through the crowd telling them that they would be leaving in six hours. Seeing Al, the two waved him to the little side room where they sat and both had a coffee in their hand.

The Captain said, "I know you are going to miss our company, but we have to shove off so that no one will know we stopped. These two days I can just account for by saying we were going a little slower than usual."

Hood said, "Me and the captain want to meet your two friends. They sound like a couple characters."

"They are that. Yeah, ok. They haven't been around humans, so it might do them some good. Be on your best behavior though, so tell them, I told you so."

The Captain replied, "Excellent. We haven't mentioned it, but do you have a load of alcohol for us for the rest of our trip?"

"Oh, yeah. I can let you have about two gallons"

"Where are you making this stuff?"

"We'll stop by on the way to the bridge and I'll show you."

"That'll be great. A still, just like the old days?"

"Sort of."

Hood said, "Let's do it."

On A Deck, Al said, "This is the still room. Go in and have a look around."

Hood opened the door and turned and asked, "What is that god awful stink?"

Al replied, "We wear hazmat suits."

"Hazmat suits? And we drank that stuff?"

"That's the fermented mash that stinks. There's nothing fun about messing with this stuff."

"Well, I've seen enough of the still room."

"Follow me," and the three walked to the bridge door and it was locked. Al said, "Ok, boys, I've frisked these two, let us in."

The door now opened and the three entered to see the backs of Legs and Ace in front of their computer monitors and Al said, "Boys, I want you to meet Hood and the Captain."

Legs and Ace swiveled their chairs and Ace asked, "Is there a protocol for meeting humans?"

"No."

"We just play it by ear?"

The Captain laughed and said to Hood, "They'll just play it by ear."

Ace asked, "Boss, are we supposed to speak proper English?"

"That was proper English."

Legs said, "Enough. What do you want?"

"These two want to see if you two can do anything but sweep floors and make beds."

Hood stammered, "No, it is isn't that at all."

Legs replied, "We know it. Boss thinks he is a vaudeville comedian. Just laugh now and then for his sake. He's easier to manage when he's happy and I'm not up to giving him another spanking."

Al said, "Spanking my ass."

"That's what I said."

Ace said, "Never mind this gentlemen, it's a twenty four seven thing."

Hood said, "Laurel and Hardy."

"Exactly."

Legs said, "One of your humans is digging around in the freight on F Deck and he pointed at the monitor. I will turn on the PA speaker for F Deck only." Having done this, Legs said into the microphone, "Decompression in ten seconds."

The captain and Hood laughed as the thief on F Deck ran for the stairway door.

The captain said to Legs and Ace, "Boys, you're my kind of people."

Legs replied, "Not really."

The Captain laughed again and said, "It was nice meeting you boys. I have to go round up that gang downstairs and get headed for Earth."

Downstairs and in the small room in the cafeteria, Hood said to Al, "We want to settle up, for all of the booze and the good time."

Al replied, "Nothing to settle."

The Captain replied, "We figure we owe you about three thousand credits."

"What in the hell am I going to do with credits? I guess, me, Legs and Ace could play cards for them."

"I see what you mean. Not many shopping malls out here. That kind of puts a damper on what me and Hood wanted to talk to you about."

"What was that?"

"I don't belong to the Corp, I'm a private contractor with my own ship. I make two trips in well over a year between Mars and Earth ferrying Corp grunts. The officers have their own fancy ship. Hood, you tell Al, it was your idea."

"Ok, Captain. Well Al, I'm getting mustered out of the Corp when I get back to Earth. The Captain here wants me to partner up with him on the Earth-Mars runs. A run once a year for him and once a year for me. There's not a whole lot of money in it, keeping the ship up eats up most of it. Anyway, I suggested to the captain that we smuggle a little booze to Mars. It's worth its weight in gold on Mars."

Al said, "That's been tried before."

"Yeah, I know it. The ships are one hundred percent clean when they leave the space ports on Earth. They have sensors that can pick booze up in a thermos bottle and they hang your ass if they find any booze. On Mars, they don't even check, no need to."

"You want me to make you the booze, right?"

"Right. One day off of our trip time to pick it up isn't noticeable. But, I see there's nothing in it for you unless it would be for attorney fees and I don't think every attorney on Earth could get you off after this hijacking thing. Well, that was our plan anyway."

Al said, "Money isn't everything you know. It is if you have some place to spend it, but I don't. I could have some for you on your next Mars run. That would be four months or so before you get here wouldn't it?"

"Yeah, a little over two months, here to Earth and back. You'll do it?"

"Two problems."

"Yes, what?"

Al said, "My partners is one problem, and the other is that is going to run me dry on mash ingredients and I'm not much on straight orange juice."

The Captain said, "You talk to Legs and Ace and if they buy in, make up a list of goods you'll need to get your shelves full again."

Al said, "I'll give it a shot. They aren't much on making moonshine. You two are taking all of the risk; the authorities can't do a damned thing to me out here."

The Captain said, "I have a handle on that. I have been getting six bottles of scotch to Mars for years. Where I hide it, that's all I can get in there. I have steady customers that know how to keep their mouths shut. How much can you let us have?"

"I have enough ingredients for about twenty gallons and that's it."

Hood looked at the Captain and laughed and said, "Twenty gallons? We're talking big money here."

The Captain said, "We're going to set up an encrypted numbered safe deposit box on Earth for you. If you ever need it, fine. Last man standing cleans it out."

Al said, "Fair enough. I'll talk it over with Legs and Ace and get in touch with you on my encrypted email account. Take it easy on the way to Earth. We don't want you getting pulled over for a DWI."

The ship undocked from the freighter and in minutes was thousands of miles away on its continued trip to Earth. On the bridge with Legs and Ace, Al watched the undocking and Ace said, "Boy, that bunch was a handful."

Al said, "Where are you getting all of these brilliant quips. A handful? That doesn't make any sense."

"You're mocking me?"

"Yes."

Ace replied, "I tried not to bruise your sensitivities by saying, humans are a pain in the ass."

"What would you know about a pain in the ass? All you have down there is a metal plate."

Legs said, "Enough. Boss, did they take all of the alcohol?"

"All except for mine."

"Oh, wonderful. I'm going to name my book, *Stranded on a Space Ship with a Lush.*"

Al replied, "I think lush is exaggerating the situation. How about social drinker?"

"Social? In your room by yourself?"

Ace said, "Sounds like a lush to me."

"Ok, lush. I've got thick skin."

"What in the hell does that mean; thick skin?"

"Ok, enough of this horseshit, partners."

Ace said, "Partners? Oh, oh, here it comes."

Legs said, "Ok, let's hear this hair brained idea."

Ace replied, "Hair brained? Where did you find that one?"

"Slang City website."

"I didn't see it."

"Under New Yorkers."

Al yelled, "For god's sake, I can't get a word in here edgewise."

Legs and Ace looked at each other and Legs mouthed *word in edgewise* to Ace as Al continued, "Here's the deal. Something I want to tell you boys. Hood or the Captain or maybe both, will be back this way in a couple months." He continued on with the lengthy story so that there would not be any misunderstandings. Al then paused, sat back in his chair and asked, "Well what do you boys think?"

Legs replied, "We listened in to your conversation."

Al yelled, "You let me ramble on for an hour telling you something you already knew?"

"You said; Something I want to tell you boys."

Ace said, "We're in. You do all the work."

Al replied, "*We're in* means *we're in*. We all do the work."

"We'll see."

"Out of curiosity, why are you in?"

Legs said, "For the experience. I'm writing a book."

"How many damned books are you writing anyway."

"Seven."

"At the same time?"

"Why not, it's just as easy as writing one."

"Forget I asked. We need a shopping list for the captain and Hood. We're never going to see the credits, so we'll order double what we need to make booze."

Legs said, "What do you mean to make booze? We have enough to make the batch for those two to take to Mars?"

"You never know."

A month later and a month before Hood and the Captain were to return, Al got an email from Hood on Earth.

"Boss.

There are three acquaintances of mine in one of those sporty and fast little jobs heading for Mars. Would it be alright if they stopped by for a drink and a quart for traveling? They're one hundred percent ok. If they weren't, I wouldn't ask. I have warned them, any funny business and the decompression thing. They are bringing some of your supplies. Downtown New Yorkers, you'll like them. They have a thing of their own down here.

Hood"

"They are bringing three old thirty eight snub-nosed for you boys. I would rather get shot than decompressed. Lol."

Al replied to Hood. *"It's your asses not ours."*

A week later, Ace said, "A ship off the beaten path heading our way. It has been cloaked until minutes ago. It's small, so it is probably your friends."

Legs said, "It's a Merlin 2500. I don't know who they are, but they have dough."

Al said, "Well, talk them in. I'll be on F Deck. I want to get those thirty-eights from them. You boys be on your toes. I'll run them through the contraband detector down there and then up to the cafeteria and then into their rooms."

"And what if you get sloppy drunk and pass out before they do?"

"Have you ever seen me sloppy drunk?"

"Yes."

The three entered from the docking bay and Al said, "Welcome gentlemen," as he was thinking, "*Well these three are right out of a mobster movie.*"

One said, "It's Boss, isn't it?"

"In name only, trust me."

"Yeah, we heard about your friends."

Al replied, "They are watching and listening to us."

Another of the three said, "The decompression thing, huh?"

"Yeah."

"Well, house rules."

Al said, "Those thirty-eight snub-nosed. I would just a soon be carrying them as you guys."

One of the three said, "Call me One. This is Two

and the short gentleman is Three. The heat is in this bag and ammo, too."

Taking the bag, Al said, "One, Two and Three, huh?"

"Have a problem with that?"

"Oh, hell no. We have a Boss, Legs and Ace here."

Two said, "We don't exist, compendia?"

"If it wasn't for your shadow, I wouldn't even know you were here. How about a Mickey Finn or a Bloody Harry?"

One said, "I hope you're talking about booze?"

"Best drinks for a million miles."

"Three of the Mickey Finns."

"Follow me gentlemen, a couple flights up. If you wouldn't mind stepping though the detector?"

Three said, "Well, they frisk us everywhere else we go, why not."

In the cafeteria with Al's guests seated, Al went to the refrigerator and retrieved four glasses already poured and set them on the table. He said, "I usually don't drink on the job, but what the hell."

Two asked, "What job? You work for somebody?"

"Just a joke, Two."

One said to Three, "This shit is better than that rot gut you make in Manhattan."

Three replied, "Hate to say it, but you're right. Must be the barley." Looking at Al, he asked, "European?"

"Not at liberty to say, Sir."

OUTER SPACE CASINO

"That's it, the barley. I knew it."

One said, "You say your android friends are watching us?"

"Yep. Ace, a little New York background music, please."

A minute passed and the sound filled the cafeteria and Al said, "Real funny, Ace. Not horns and sirens, *music*."

One said, "A couple characters alright. Tell Ace to leave that on. That damned Merlin 2500 is so quiet it drives you nuts. Besides, it reminds me of the old days. There hasn't been a car in New York City in thirty years. Got those damned little things that run on a rail everywhere."

Two said, "This stuff has a bite to it, but not so bad I won't have another."

Al asked, "Another all around?"

They all agreed and Al brought a pitcher and poured four more and said, "Two is my limit. We run a tight ship here. Will you be spending the night? The accommodations aren't much. Nothing but crew quarters."

Three replied, "I can live without that. A couple more drinks and we'll spend the night in the Merlin and shove off in eight or ten hours. Want to stay on the Mar's radar so to speak. We'll come in and meet your partners before we leave."

"They'll be tickled."

"I bet. You have that gallon of booze for us."

119

"I thought it was a quart."

"This is not one quart booze. What do we owe you?"

"Three snub-nosed thirty eights."

Two said, "Those were a bitch to come by. Hell, they must be over two hundred years old and the shells too. Got them from an antique dealer in the Bronx. Made him an offer he couldn't refuse. Shoot at your own risk."

Over the PA speaker, Legs said, "You can't shoot a pistol in a space ship."

Al yelled, "No shit, Legs."

One said, "Well, lead us out of here. Walking through that freight is like a maze. You know you have a fortune here in freight, and no one would buy it."

"I suppose, but I'm not going to starve to death."

Hours later on the bridge, Legs said to Al, "Well, your boys are up and heading for the cafeteria. They even went through the contraband detector."

"I'll go get them. They want to meet you two, but I don't know why. They could talk to that refrigerator down there."

"They want to, because someone on this ship has to be smarter than you."

Ace said, "Those are some shady characters. One, Two and Three, can you believe it? I wonder what their story is."

Al replied, "None of our business."

"You can say that again."

In the cafeteria, Al and his guests had some black coffee with a shot of alcohol in it and One said to Al, "We were never here, right?"

"Right. How is New York City getting along?"

"Just like always. Some of the people living in ivory towers and the rest didn't change much in a couple hundred years or so. Hell, most of the people are living in places that old. They just keep patching them up."

"Is the Shilo Bar still open?"

"Oh, hell yes, Two runs some booze through there and I have some games. It's a cash cow. Have to pay off the surveillance camera people, but we have always had to pay off somebody. We have a meet on Mars with the cartel. Long story. We get caught on Mars and we're toast. You're looking at three school teachers on a foreign exchange thing. Well, let's go meet your boys, we have to get out of here."

"Well, boys, here we are. You know who these three are. Gentlemen, the one with the red dot is Ace, blue dot Legs."

One said, "I've heard about you two."

Ace said, "Nothing good I suppose, we're androids."

"On the contrary. I heard you two were the brains of this outfit."

"Well, you know how to New York sweet talk."

Legs said, "In all honesty, Boss does all of the

thinking and we just say bullshit."

"Whatever works. That's some good booze you're making."

"Obviously we have to thank out resident alcoholic for that."

Two said, "I see what you mean Al, about these two. Reminds me of my two brothers."

Three said, "We have something for you boys. A movie. Same place we got the thirty eights. Was never shown. The New York gangs put a freeze on it. We put it on a flash drive for you."

Ace asked, "We have never seen it?"

"Nope. I did, and it was ok."

One said, "Ok, we're out of here. We have people to see. We'll see you on the way back to Earth."

Hours later, Legs said, "We'll see you on the way back to Earth? What in the hell are we running here a Route 71 flop house?"

Al replied, "Well, they did bring some sugar and malt."

"Whoopie do. Do I like sugar and malt? I don't know. I might if I could taste and eat."

"Always negative, aren't you, Legs?"

"Only when it's warranted. Let's watch that new movie."

Ace said, "I'm up for that."

Al said, "Wait a minute, I'm going to mix a drink."

Legs replied, "Be sure and mark it on your chart."

Al mumbled, "Rules are rules."

Ace said, "That's the best gangster movie I've seen."

Legs replied, "That's because you haven't seen it ten times before. What is the point of being the big cheese and wealthy, if you get killed when you're twenty five?"

Ace said, "We're only nine. Twenty five sounds old to me."

Al replied, "Yeah, it was pretty good. Did you notice the thirty eight Blackie had? Hell, it might be the same one I have. Speaking of that, is it necessary for you two to carry them in your pockets? Who are you going to shoot?"

Ace replied, "I feel naked without it."

"Aw, horse shit. You heard Cagney say that."

"There's no shells in it. That's a new rule, no shells in guns."

Al said, "I've got a new rule. It's Ace's turn to bottle the booze."

"It's not my turn."

"Yes it is. You put the stuff that's in the big thing into the little things."

"You had better write that down for me. If we give all of the booze to Hood and the Captain, what are we going to do about the gangsters on their way back from Mars?"

Al replied, "I have some stashed away."

Legs said, "I bet you do. Is there any way we could rig up an intravenous system for you so you won't have to wash all of those glasses?"

"Who washes glasses?"

Al had been in touch with Hood on the internet and Hood and the Captain would be at the freighter in four days, along with twenty Corp troops and the freight Hood had promised to deliver.

Legs said to Al, "There's no way in hell that all of these humans can be showing up here without word getting to the space ports."

"Not our problem. Hood and the Captain seem to know what they're doing. It's probably a one shot deal selling the booze. It's a quick turnaround for them on Mars and they'll be gone before word gets out and they won't have any booze on board when they get back to Earth."

Ace said, "I could make a movie about this?"

Al asked, "How is your other movie coming along?"

"Finishing touches."

"What color are the androids?"

Legs said, "What color are the androids?"

Ace replied, "The one that I call Boss, is pink. I had to use one of your wanted poster pictures for the facial features."

"Are you going to bottle that alcohol or not?"

"On my way."

Legs said to Al, "The Captain is cloaking."

"How far out?"

"Six hours."

Al said, "I'll wander down and get the cafeteria all set up. Those troops can make up their own beds. It won't be the first time they crawled into a bed someone had left all messed up."

Legs replied, "I think most of that last bunch slept on the floor where they passed out."

"Well, at least they slept, that's something you two don't do. By the way, how many movies do you watch a day anyway?"

Ace replied, "Rarely more than ten. We just watched "*PEARL HARBOR*." The guy that wrote that had an imagination."

Al replied, "That really happened."

"It really happened?"

"Yes."

"They didn't put that in our memory banks."

"Now why in the hell would they? They didn't put James Cagney in there either."

Legs asked, "How about "*KING KONG*," was that bullshit?"

"Yeah."

"How are we supposed to know the difference? Most things that humans actually do are bullshit."

Al said, "That's beside the point. You guys figure it out, I'm going downstairs."

On the PA system came, "Boss?"

"Yeah."

"Twenty minutes."

"Ok, I'm on F Deck now."

"I know you're on F Deck, I can see you."

"Well, what am I doing?"

"Giving me the finger.   You had better have them all go through the contraband detector, I'm a little nervous about this bunch."

Al said, "Well, that would be a first for an erector set, getting nervous."

Ace said, "Is erector set, some kind of racial slur?"

Al replied, "Yes."

The Captain's ship docked with the freighter and in minutes Hood and the Captain entered F Deck, followed by about twenty Corp troops.

Al said, "This bunch looks like they are a little green behind the ears."

The Captain replied, "Right out of Corp camp."

The boys want them to go through the detector. The space ports and the Corp might try to pull a fast one."

"No problem."

Al said to Hood, "A new uniform?"

"Yeah, a commercial uniform. First mate."

The Captain said, "You boys go on ahead. I'll take care of this bunch. Ace and Legs have eyes on us don't they?"

"You can count on it."

"Go ahead then."

With the troops in the cafeteria pouring Mickey Finns from the jars, Al, the Captain and Hood sat in the small room discussing their business arrangement and the Captain said, "All of your goods are in my ship and we'll unload before we leave. Is the alcohol ready?"

Al replied, "Yes, we have put it in five gallon plastic containers."

"How much?"

"Thirty gallons, and I ran bone dry on ingredients."

"Well, you aren't now. I had to lie like hell on the weight of those troops out there and their supplies. They left with empty packs, but I can take care of that on Mars."

Over the PA system was Legs, "What about those troops out there? Are we going to be front page news?"

Hood replied, "Must be legs, huh? These troops have a code of their own. They don't rat out each other. Some didn't want to stop, but I don't see any out there with empty glasses."

Legs replied, "Fine, it's your ass."

"We have it covered. Is that all, Legs?"

"No. New rule. No shells in guns."

"We don't have any guns."

"How do I know that, you and the Captain didn't go through the detector."

Al yelled, "For god's sake Legs, they aren't packin."

"Ace will be down with a hand held."

The Captain said, "A tight ship, I like it."

Al asked, "This is a one shot deal on the booze then, huh?"

"We'll see how it goes. That's a lot of freight; do you want it upstairs or on F Deck?"

"F Deck. We have a small elevator if we need any of it."

Hood said, "How were my friends that dropped by? Any problems?"

"One, Two and Three?"

"If that's what they used for their handles, yes."

"No problems. Typical downtown New York City gangsters."

"They're business men."

"That's what I said."

Hood replied, "There may be a few friends from Mars stop by on the way to Earth."

"Can they keep their mouths shut?"

"They have to, they're politicians."

"Politicians?"

"And a couple judges. All good people."

"Hell, I've got gangsters going to be here sometime."

"It won't be an issue if it happens, they know each other."

Al replied, "You two make yourself at home and we'll load and unload your ship in ten hours or so."

The Captain replied, "Fine. Pour me another one of those."

On the bridge with Al, Legs yelled, "We'll see how it goes?"

Ace followed with, "There may be a few friends from Mars stop by on the way to Earth? What in the hell is this? Are we going to have to build a revolving door down there on F Deck?"

Legs said, "What do you think you have here, a couple sweatshop slaves."

Al replied, "Sorry, boys. Things have just got a little out of hand."

"A little?"

"Yeah, a little. It's no big deal; we don't have anything to do anyway."

"You mean, you don't. We're on fire watch."

"Fire watch? We have heat and smoke detectors all over the place and automatic Nitrogen gas fire extinguishers."

"Yes, but we have to alert the ship and maintain crowd control."

"Alert the ship and crowd control my ass. You two set for months watching surveillance monitors where nothing happens. It's understandable though with your picks of movies."

"Well, that's better than looking at the bottom of a Mickey Finn glass."

Al said, "Ok, ok, enough bullshit. I'll see if I can ratchet this down a bit."

Ace said, "I would think so. Me and Legs are going

to have to talk this over."

Al replied, "During a movie or in-between movies. I've created a couple monsters."

"I saw it. Abbot and Costello, *"FRANKENSTEIN."*

Ten hours and the Captain and Hood stopped by for a Bloody Harry. When able, the troops unloaded and loaded the captain's ship and the Captain's ship was on its way back to the space traffic lane between Earth and Mars.

Legs said to Al, "Well, how did the ratcheting go?"

"Didn't have time to discuss it. We can talk on their way back when they and the changed out troops stop for a drink."

"Good work. You are a natural manager. Ace and I have something we want to discuss with you and it will take a while, so go get a Mickey Finn."

Frowning, Al said, "That serious, huh? I'm going to the broom closet?"

"That was our first choice, but us three will have to vote on that. we'll see how it goes."

CHAPTER FIVE

LAS VEGAS

With drink in hand, Al said, "Ok, shoot."

Ace said, "I don't have any shells. I've been dry firing a lot though."

Legs said, "Attention. Boss, have you heard of Las Vegas?"

Al replied, "In the radiation zone. Hot as hell and no water. Never been there of course, no one has for a hundred years."

"The history of Las Vegas?"

"Some. What I saw in a couple gangster movies,

that's about it. Out in the middle of nowhere."

Legs replied, "Does that ring a bell?"

Al looked puzzled for a moment and replied, "Like us. In the middle of nowhere. Like Las Vegas, in-between all of the big cities. Is this a book you're writing?"

"Yes."

"Ok, go ahead."

Ace said, "Las Vegas was out in the middle of nowhere because they could offer services not available in the big cities. At least not quality services. Bottom line is, they made a shit pot full of money doing it."

Al said, "Just a minute," and he finished his drink and smiled and then said, "You boys are geniuses. Las Vegas in space. If we charge these troops for their drinks, we'll have ourselves a nice little speakeasy here."

Legs replied, "We're thinking bigger."

Al laughed and said, "You've been watching those twentieth century casino movies. How much bigger?"

Ace said, "The whole damned ship. Bars, casinos, rooms, restaurant, the whole ball of wax."

Still laughing, Al said, "I'm in, but how in the hell are we going to pull this off? We don't have any credits. That would take a fortune."

Ace said, "We trade the cargo in the freighter to the space ports for the freighter. It's not a good deal for them, but it's better than no freighter and no cargo. That will get them off our ass."

Al said, "Ok, the money?"

"Investors, and we can learn from Las Vegas. No gangsters. What is our share of the booze Hood and the captain just left with?"

"I don't know. A drop in the bucket though. It's a great idea you two. We can see already that what we're doing now is going to spiral out of control. How many commercial and private ships pass by us in twenty four hours?"

Legs replied, "Four to ten. About four hundred humans."

"Hell, I bet there would be ships coming directly here just for the booze."

Ace said, "And the gambling."

"Gambling?"

"Yeah, like those machines in *"GOODFELLAS."* We have slot machine internet programs. We can rig them up on monitors. Same thing."

"Boys?"

"What?"

"Why are you wanting to do this? Now me, it's just the thrill of the game. I don't have any more use for credits and money than you do?"

Legs replied, "We want to buy androids going out of service and we want six right away."

"Well, that's understandable by human standards, but what's the connection between you and other androids?"

"There isn't any. It's a matter of rebellion I guess.

At one time we thought nothing of being dismantled for scrap, but now we do. I guess it's the Frankenstein in us."

"So, it will be me and a ship full of androids?"

"Yes. We don't trust humans."

"I can live with that setup. Finally something we agree on. We are going to have to pencil this whole thing out if we are going to raise the money from investors. Right off, we're going to have to make the booze here on the ship. It's not allowed on Mars and can't be shipped off the Earth."

How to remodel the inside of a space ship to look and function like a casino was not something available on the internet. There hadn't been a casino on Mars, the Moon or Earth for over a hundred years, so there wasn't much on casinos at all. The three watched the old twentieth century Las Vegas movies and captured still pictures which they examined methodically. Immediately the obvious problem confronted them pertaining to the project and that was what they didn't have and how they were going to get it there. Weight was a big issue and water was of great importance. They would have rooms for rent and space ships had used dry waterless showers for decades, so that was not an issue. Most of the water could be recycled like on Mars and the Moon, but the initial volume of water for making alcohol drinks and water consumption would be considerable.

All of the construction materials would be of graphene and carbon so the walls would only be an eighth of an inch thick and rigid and light.

The three kept adding items to the list and making sketches and had a rough idea what the inside of the ship would consist of. Instead of the six existing high ceiling elevations of the ship, there would be twelve elevations or floors. These would consist of rooms to rent, a large restaurant, bar and entertainment, and floors of gambling devices.

The top level originally being the bridge and officer's quarters, would be the same, but would include equipment for the manufacture of alcohol. A Deck 1 and A Deck 2 would also be office space and living quarters for management of the space ship casino and a maintenance shop and everything else required to operate the casino.

Their planning was interrupted by the three New York gangsters coming back from Mars and now accompanied by some lady friends. There were a few awkward moments for Al as Legs and Ace watched the surveillance cameras and shook their heads and said, "Boss, are you watching this?"

"No."

Hood and the Captain showed up with another load of troops and spent enough time there for the troops to get drunk and left with a gallon of alcohol. Nothing about the Las Vegas project was mentioned to them, because the planning hadn't been completed yet.

Then it was the politicians and judges and Al recognized most of them on sight. Legs and Ace took care of these people while Al stayed out of sight. Twenty four hours later they departed to the relief of the three."

Al said, "You realize they drank all of the damned alcohol don't you?"

Legs said, "Oh, no, what are we going to do, kill ourselves."

"Two out of three would be a good start."

The planning continued and resulted in one of the computers full of spreadsheets, accurate engineering drawings and a large batch of mash had been set to fester. Some private stock for Boss.

Al said to Legs and Ace, "Well, what do you think? Do we have everything covered?"

Ace replied, "Yes, but the bottom line number is staggering."

Legs said, "Over four million credits."

"Well, we ran the numbers. If the joint runs at half capacity, we can pay dividends to the shareholders. Over that is gravy. Those passenger ships take two months to get to Mars. By the time they get here they'll pay anything to have a little fun. Have you boys done all of the calculations so that we can stay between Earth and Mars?"

Ace said, "The flight controls have been set and programmed. The ship will continue to move every two weeks to keep aligned. For three months the damned sun will be between us and Mar and shut the traffic down and we are coming up on that in about thirty days."

Al replied, "That will work out fine if we can get what we need up here to start remodeling. I guess we make the call, huh?"

"Go for it."

After a night's sleep for Boss, he sat at his bridge computer and sent an encrypted email to Hood on Earth.

"Hood

We have a business proposal for you to examine. It will require your help on Earth to put this deal together. I will be transmitting you all of our documents and drawings concerning the deal and a full explanation. The project is called Las Vegas. Give me a heads up on your thoughts after you examine the proposal. Regardless, on your next trip by, I need you to bring six model RTR used androids. They are being taken out of service and should be cheap by android standards. These out of the booze money, past and future.

Boss"

After all of this was sent to Hood, Al said, "Well, we might as well drop the hammer on the space port people about this ship and their cargo."

Legs replied, "They're going to be pissed. Think they'll make a move on us?"

"Could be. Is the cloaking device working ok?"

"Yes."

"If we see anything fishy heading our way, we'll cloak. They can't board us if they can't see us."

"What are we going to do about offloading this cargo to their freighter if they go for the deal?"

"Very carefully and no androids, you can't trust em. They do everything you tell them."

Legs replied, "Well, we're evidence of that or we wouldn't even be involved in your crazy deal."

"My crazy deal?"

"And do something about that mash, I can smell it all the way in here."

The space ports agreed to the deal quickly and Al said "Well, the ship is legally ours now, but they can steal it from us just like we stole it from them. There wasn't much doubt about them accepting our deal."

Ace said, "We are going to have to keep on our toes.."

Al said, "You don't have toes?"

"Why would I have toes?"

"Whatever. I had better work on that still design. We need a big still."

Legs asked, "How big?"

"Big enough so that we aren't making it all of the time. The three months the Earth and Mars positions are where there is no space traffic, we can stockpile it. Let's say five thousand gallons of mash fermenting at a time."

"Five thousand gallons?"

"Yeah. Run the numbers. Every yahoo that stops here drinks continuously and then has to have a couple bottles for the trip home."

Legs asked, "Where in the hell are we going to get that much water?"

Ace said, "Boss, I've got an idea."

"Well, let's hear it."

"A bottle and water deposit."

Al asked, "What in the hell does that mean?"

"Every one that shows up has to have a couple bottles full of water as a deposit for what they drink and leave with. Humans had bottle deposits in America for a while when all of the good beach sand was covered with water. No water in them then of course, but that's no big deal."

Al replied, "I think you're on to something there, numbskull. We have five thousand gallons aboard right now and we'll order some more to get by. We have enough extra ingredients we ordered to get a batch going."

"That'll cost an arm and a leg for the water."

"Cost of doing business, boys."

Legs said, "If there is a business. Nothing from Hood on the deal, huh?"

"Nope. The space port freighter will be here in three

weeks. I hope we didn't get the cart in front of the horse."

Ace said, "That's a new one. Don't tell me, let me think on it."

Finally the email came from Hood. Al, Legs and Ace had it on their monitors and put it on audio.

"Boss and the boys
The captain and I have been through all of your paperwork and it's a bang up idea, in theory anyway. We crunched all of the numbers," and Ace broke in, "They destroyed our calculations?" Legs said, "Shut up, Ace." *The captain and I decided that this kind of a project is cost prohibitive because it would cost millions of credits on a gamble. That is too much capital to be raised from investors on a gamble that may be against the law. When this was decided and as a last ditch effort, I contacted a shyster lawyer I know and discussed it with him. He went through the books and after several days he contacted us and said that there isn't legally a damned thing the authorities on Earth or Mars can do to prevent such a venture. He also said, if it wasn't so costly, he would invest in it. Hell, the Captain and I would too, but we don't have that kind of money. The people that do, don't want to be involved in something of this sort or they are the kind of people you mentioned that you don't want involved. So we just dropped it. The lawyer called back and asked why we didn't float it on the New York Stock Exchange.*

I asked if that was legal and he said, Hell yes, its legal. A high risk stock for a lot of little people and if it goes bust, no one gets hurt that bad. If you are interested, I will do the leg work on Earth with some people I know. I don't know shit about the stock market or how it works. If it all came together it would take a few people to get everything set up and they would have to do it on a contingency basis for a piece of the action. You boys talk it over and get back to me.

Hood and the Captain"

The three paused for a moment digesting what they had heard and Al said, "That's really sounds awfully complicated to me."

Legs replied, "Everything is awfully complicated for you."

"Well, I could ask you two electric toasters to do the thinking for me."

Ace replied, "Good idea."

Al said, "You know our motto. What in the hell do we have to lose? I'm up for giving it a shot. There isn't a damned thing we can do here right now. We are going to have to have Hood and the Captain do everything on Earth for us."

Legs said, "They'll have to have a piece of the action."

Al said, "I don't know shit, but I know we have to keep fifty one percent of this deal."

"Well, he's your human friend. Get on the horn and

sweet talk him."

"Ok, but I have to warn you, he's just an everyday New York street hustler."

"Perfect."

After days of email communications, there was a plan. For a piece of the action, Hood and the Captain would open an office in downtown New York City. Their shares to be depending on the capital raised and the success of the project, but a fair amount. They would do whatever was necessary to get the ball rolling. Deals would be made with stock brokers, attorneys and others to get capital and start buying and shipping materials. Down the road, Hood and the Captain would handle all reservations and communications with the space casino that was to be named Las Vegas. Of primary concern was the purchase and delivering of construction materials to Las Vegas, along with twenty additional androids. The six already ordered would be dropped off by a friend on his way to Mars.

The space port freighter had arrived and the gravity setting was reduced on both ships so the moving of cargo was manageable from one ship to the other through the large docking ports of both ships. As planned, there was no communication between Al and the space port people during the transfer and he, Legs and Ace watched carefully on surveillance camera monitors.

Down on the lower decks, Al said, "This thing looks huge inside with all of the cargo gone."

Legs replied, "I think we had better spend some time studying how to work with that graphene and epoxy."

"I hope your android friends know something about it, because we don't."

"Yeah, maybe they had two jobs. Flying spaceships and gluing graphene walls together in their off hours."

Al replied, "Like walking and chewing gum."

"What in the hell does that mean? What's gum? It'll take a month to teach the androids your language."

"You mean to tell me, they are going to be as dumb as you two?"

Ace said, "We could have you teach them something, but that would be putting the cart before the horse."

"Cute, Ace."

Al drew up plans for two rooms on A Deck; one for mash and one for a huge still. One of the small rooms with metal walls on A Deck would be sealed and the entire room filled with mash mixture. Parts were listed for the still and it looked a little unconventional, but would work fine. It was not rocket science.

An email from Hood:

"You boys owe us a shit pot full of money. Lawyers, bribes, accountants and not to mention six androids and you are wrong, they aren't cheap. The New York Stock Exchange deal is in the works and stock being

allocated. Now all we have to do is sell it. A million shares and twenty thousand going on the market at five credits a share. The accountant said that these will be bought at increasing prices. And more shares go on the market later. We had to give stock options to associates to buy at the market price when bought. My shyster lawyer said that it's going to be a runaway market. This being the case, construction materials are being purchased on credit and that is money we don't have. If this deal goes sour, there will be two more humans living on that freighter. The six androids and some miscellaneous are on the way now. Hopefully all of the construction materials will be sent the minute the stock hits the market."

*"You should have enough to keep you busy remodeling through the blackout period, (**The blackout period is about three months per Earth year when there is no travel or freight between Mars and Earth. Having different orbits around the sun, during these three months the Earth and Mars are too far apart for travel and even reliable telecommunications**.)*

*"The Captain is giving up the troop transport business and working on this full time. His ship might be a nice little fun flight job. Found a cheap used commercial 3D Printer on the Moon. That will come in handy for you. You are front page news again. **Gangster opens Las Vegas casino in space.** New Yorkers are loving it.*

Hood and the Captain."

Al said, "Well boys, it looks like it's a go. Let's start marking on the walls of the decks where the partitions are going to be. If we get those androids trained up and they know where the walls will go, we can turn them loose and we can start on everything else. With twenty more after these six, it'll keep us busy keeping them working. I guess I'll be the general foreman."

Legs said, "That's bullshit."

"You're the general foreman, Legs."

"Why me?"

"Because you couldn't keep quiet. Never look a gift horse in the mouth."

Ace said, "Don't tell me, don't tell me."

Legs said to Ace, "Get Boss on the PA. An email for him."

Al replied to the PA speaker, "Be there in a minute."

In five minutes, Al was at his monitor and opened the email.

"Boss.

Bad news. Our mutual friend, One, called. He said the Corp at the space port on Mars has a drone on the way to your location. It left Mars after the freight was transferred to the space port freighter. As he understood it, coming from a friend in high places, the drone is to attach to your hull and through the Drisdell vent check valves, inject an odorless lethal gas.

Apparently to kill you and then negotiate with the androids to surrender the ship. There is nothing we can do on this end to help you. We could not get there in time. The drone is operating on frequency 197.044. There is no way to tell when it will arrive. You have hazmat suits, so I would suggest putting one on right now. Good luck.

Hood."

Al said, "Well, hell. You heard him boys. Get your hazmat suits."

Ace replied, "Now why would we do that?"

"Lethal gas."

"Lethal for you. Any gas that would harm us would also make the controls and electronics on this ship useless. It would never make it to Mars or the Earth."

"Well then, its hazmat time for me. I guess I'm supposed to live the rest of my life in a hazmat suit. Hell, they could pump that gas in here for years."

Legs said, "Well, we can't just leave here with the ship. That drone will just catch up to us, they are super-fast."

"What in the hell is a Drisdell vent check valve?"

"It is part of the temperature control. It dissipates the internal air that continually increases in temperature due to the nuclear reactor and goes through an external heat exchanger."

Al asked, "Can we plug it up or shut it off?"

"Not from inside the ship and if you could you

would be dead in an hour and us in two days."

"Well shit. What's plan B then?"

Legs asked, "What was plan A?"

"The vent."

"Then its plan B, I guess."

"And what's that?"

"Give them the freighter or destroy the drone."

Al said, "The only way they are going to get this freighter is up their ass."

"Then we destroy the drone or its game over."

"Well, you think on it while I go get in a hazmat suit."

Lumbering back in a hazmat suit, Al asked, "Ok, what have you got for me?"

Legs replied, "There are seventeen possibilities and they are listed on your monitor. It is essential that it be a total surprise and a clean kill. The pros and cons of all seventeen options are described."

Al read from the seemingly endless list and said, "I like number ten, but I don't understand it. You have it listed as a five star rating. That's better than most. Ok, explain it to me."

Ace replied, "With power cables from the nuclear generator, we electrify the Drisdell vents. There are only two. When contact is made with the Drisdell vents, a charge of five thousand amps will be transferred to the drone. This will electronically fry it and conceivably blow a few holes in it. The cables will have to be attached externally."

"You mean out there?"

"Out there."

Al said, "Well, hell. There is one emergency space suit on board, I guess I'm up."

Legs said, "You are too valuable."

"What does that mean?"

"It means you don't know what the hell you're doing. You couldn't find a Drisdell vent check valve if it was in your bunk with you."

Ace added, "Let alone hook up the power cables."

Legs said, "We are designed for decompression, but can't tolerate the outside temperature, so Ace or I will have to use the space suit. You would run out of oxygen anyway."

"I guess we had better get started, huh?"

Ace replied, "Yes. The vents are below F Deck and near the reactor generator. Let's round up the cables and tools and get them to F Deck."

Three hours later, Legs in the space suit was outside the ship and Al and Ace could not see what he was doing. They had him on their PA speakers, but that was about it and Legs wasn't saying anything. Another two hours and Legs asked to be let in the air lock.

Al asked, "Well?"

"It'll either work or it won't. I didn't want to be out there when we energize the cables. If they are somehow grounded to the ship, we are in big trouble."

"Oh, great. How much trouble?"

"You won't need an air lock to get outside."

"Seriously?"

Legs answered, "If we bring the power up slow we should be able to tell if there is a problem before it's critical. If everything is ok, we have to leave the power on to the Drisdell vents."

Now back on the bridge, Ace said, "I'm bringing up the power and we're going to lose power on a lot of stuff in the ship."

Ace counted out the numbers of amps as the power level increased and the first thing to go was the lighting system. With emergency battery lamps on, the power was increased and the surveillance cameras were lost. Throughout the ship, systems were going down. Power to the crews quarters, refrigerators and air conditioners, but at five thousand amps there had been no damage to the ship. The three sat in a dimly lit bridge with computers and monitors down, but emergency controls now operated one computer and one monitor.

Al said, "This could get real boring real quick. Hell, they might not be here for a week. Whether they are cloaked or not, we won't know they are out there. We don't even know if this damned thing will work."

Legs said, "You could go out there with a lightbulb and check it."

"Six more coming just like you guys, huh?"

"Oh, no. We'll have to train them up to our level.

All we can do is teach them everything we know."

"And what the hell is that?"

"What we know is, if Boss says it, its bullshit."

"I couldn't hire one drinking buddy for this ship? That was too much to ask?"

Legs relied, "Yes. No sense in throwing good money after bad."

Al replied, "You know those big machines where they drop stuff into and it shreds them?"

"Yes."

"That's where you two would be if it wasn't for me."

Legs replied, "I hope I wired up those vents right and it doesn't blow the side out of this ship. We should have had you do it."

Ace said, "Boys, boys, enough. We're screwed. No internet. No movies. What do we do now Legs, sit here and talk to Al for days on end?"

Legs answered, "That shredder sounds better all the time."

Al asked, "Do I have to keep wearing this damned hazmat suit?"

"Not if our trap works."

"Meaning, yes, huh?"

"You never know."

Four days passed as the three sat on the bridge and Al was looking a little haggard through the face plate of the Hazmat suit. He said to the two, "Can you imagine trying to sleep in this damned thing?"

Ace replied, "I can't even imagine trying to sleep."

"Well, it's no piece of cake in this suit, I can tell you that."

Legs replied, "That doesn't make any sense."

"Yeah, you probably don't even know what cake is."

"No, the, *I can tell you that.* You just did tell us that."

The freighter shuddered and there was a loud hum reverberating through the hull. This was followed by two rumbling thuds and Legs said, "I think we had a nibble."

The lights came on and monitors lit up and Legs yelled to Ace, "Damage assessment?"

Ace replied quickly, "No damage to the hull and no atmosphere lost."

Legs said to Al, "Well, Boss, there you go. A little android ingenuity."

Ace said, "Blew the breaker. The cables out there are dead. I want to go out and see what we did to that drone."

"Be my guest. Disconnect everything and bring the cables in, we may be needing them."

Al was taking off the hazmat suit and said, "It smells as bad in that suit as it does in the mash room."

Legs replied, "Same process."

"Whatever. I need a cold Mickey Finn."

"Good luck on that. The refrigerators and freezers have been off for four days."

"Well, a warm Mickey Finn then."

Ace said, "Get me a jug of water. I'll take it outside for a minute and it'll be frozen solid."

Al said, "Always thinking, aren't you, Ace."

"Somebody has to do it."

"I guess. If that drone is out there, see if there is anything we can use off of it."

"I seriously doubt if there's a bottle of booze on it."

"You never know."

After his ice project, Ace made his way to the drone that was just coming into the sun on the slow revolving freighter. The drone was about thirty feet long and there were several holes in its hull where the metal had melted. Other than that it, looked in good shape and was attached to the freighter by clamp devices that had grabbed the Drisdell vents. When close to the drone and near one of the holes in its hull, the faceplate of the space suit flashed a toxic gas warning. A manual lever released the clamps from the Drisdell vents and with a leg; Ace pushed the drone slowly away from the freighter. By the time he had retrieved the cables and reached the airlock door, the dead drone was fifty feet from the freighter and moving slowly away.

Inside, Legs asked, "Poison gas?"

"Yes. Holes in the hull of the drone."

"Well, the drone isn't cloaked now. Mars will see it leaving and know we destroyed it, but won't know how. No reason another attempt would be any more successful. That unmanned drone probably cost as much as this freighter."

Al said, "Well, let's hope this is the end of it. It's not likely they will advertise that they lost another ship. I think I'll celebrate with a Bloody Harry on ice."

They went back to the bridge and Al sent Hood an email, "*We're back on track.*"

Legs said, "Another one of those fast little space jobs heading this way."

Al replied, "Are you sure it isn't another drone?"

"Yes, they sent a transmission to Earth before leaving the traffic lane."

"What was it?"

"To someone named Lolita and the kids. Do you know her?"

"Now, why would I know Lolita and the kids?"

Legs replied, "You never know."

"What's their ETA?"

"Little over an hour."

Al said, "I'll be on F Deck. Keep an eye on us."

"Roger that."

"Roger that?"

Ace said, "*BOMBER COMMAND.*"

"On their way in, Boss," and out of the airlock came a man in a Corp uniform and plodding behind him while looking at the floor came six androids identical to Ace and Legs.

Over the PA came Legs saying, "They look a little green behind the ears."

The man in uniform asked, "Who was that? I thought you were alone."

"I am. That was an android."

"An android that can talk? Never heard of it. New model?"

"Yeah."

The man said, "Well, these aren't and you don't have to worry about them talking. They just sit and stare at a monitor twenty four hours a day. I'm a major; we will just leave it at that. Where do you want this bunch?"

"I'll take care of it. Are you staying over?"

"No."

"How about a drink of the best booze in the galaxy?"

"Don't drink."

"Well, is there anything I can do for you before you leave?"

The Major replied, "Yes. Who let you out of that locked cabin on the transport ship to Earth?"

"No one sir, I picked the lock."

"You can't pick an electromagnetic lock."

Al replied, "Thanks to James Cagney I could."

"Is he in the Corp?"

"No, just a friend. Trust me, Sir, no Corp man helped me."

"That's good enough for me. I'll be on my way.

Getting these androids wherever you want them, is going to be like trying to herd cats."

"I hear ya."

When the Major had left for his ship, Al said, "Can you communicate with these contraptions?"

Ace replied, "We have been. It's androids to you. That's no way to start a close relationship."

Legs added, "And you talk about dumb, they don't know anything."

Al replied, "Well, that rings a bell? Get them up to the bridge. Do we have six monitors?"

"We have eight, but only four are operational."

"Looking at this bunch, I don't think it will make any difference. They just need something to stare at."

Ace said, "Now, that was uncalled for."

Legs said, "Ok, Bossman, but don't forget your black whip."

"Funny."

On the bridge, Al was right. Four of the androids stared at a black screen and Al said to Ace and Legs, "Alright you two, whip them into shape."

Ace said to Legs, "I think *"WHITE HEAT,"* and two of them can double up on a monitor."

Al replied, "Oh, great, we're going to have six more movie junkies."

"They're going to be learning English."

"Well, *excuuuse* me. I'm going to check that batch

of mash."

Legs said to Al, "I thought all humans were drunks. Did I hear that major right?"

Al replied, "I think he has head problems. I'm going below and make some measurements and see what I can salvage for the still."

An email came in from Hood saying, "*The Las Vegas stock was truly a runaway in the stock exchange and was now trading at twenty seven credits and change. Fifty thousand more shares were issued and were expected to sell at about fifty credits a share. This covered the cost of two freighter deliveries of construction materials we sent and twenty more androids and parts. They will get there under the wire on the blackout period and left Earth a couple weeks ago. We have a lot of balls in the air down here. Before long, telecommunication with you will be interrupted by the Sun, so if I don't hear from you right away, I will in three months. The freighters will have to set out the blackout period at your location for three months plus. You don't have to worry about the crews drinking your booze; your junk androids we bought are flying the ships. We'll get the freighters back here somehow.*"

Almost two weeks passed and the Las Vegas was in the blackout period when Ace said, "Two ships in the traffic lane for Mars. They should make their turn any time."

The two ships made the turn and would be at the Las Vegas within hours.

Al said, "Your boys are coming along fine. They learned some kind of English in a matter of hours, but I think a better choice of movies would have helped. We need to do something with those uniforms and your cousins need names. How about one through six?"

Legs replied, "Oh, here we go. They are just numbers to you."

"Ok, Mr. politically correct. Name them, but don't expect me to remember their names."

Ace replied, "Me and Legs already thought about this. We are going to dye their hats different colors. There is dye in the laundry. Bleach the hats out and color them. We'll have a green, blue, red, yellow, black and white hats. That's their names. Do you think if you saw one of them wearing a red hat you would know what his name is?"

"Yeah, smartass, unless they change hats."

Ace said, "Now why in the hell would they do that? They wouldn't know who they were."

Al replied, "I don't know, just a thought. We'll try it."

"Try it? You aren't dealing with a bunch of your drunken buddies here."

"That's one reason I don't trust them."

"Well, you always have your black whip."

Al replied, "Whatever. Get them off of those

damned movies and it's all hands on F Deck. There is no one to unload those freighters, but us. Set gravity about twenty percent."

Legs said, "Roger that."

"And tell the rainbow boys, to get the graphene material, epoxy and other androids first."

"Rainbow boys?"

"How about knuckleheads?"

"We'll go with rainbow boys."

Al continued, "As soon as it is unloaded, the rainbow boys can start home schooling the twenty androids."

"We need more monitors."

"There are hundreds of them somewhere for the slot machines on one of those freighters. I'll find the monitors"

Ace said, "They can only dock one freighter at a time. I'll have them dock the freighter with the monitors. I have already received their ship's manifests and there are graphene panels and epoxy on both ships."

Legs said, "That's the plan then. The rainbow boys get the androids on the computer training and come back down and help with the unloading."

Al asked, "Now, what's wrong with that plan?"

Legs replied, "One of them may be a Corp plant and activate the ship's computer?"

"And?"

We already thought of that. We rigged it so it can't

happen."

"You might have said something, but that's still not good enough for me."

Ace said, "I'll babysit."

Everything went as planned with a few hiccups and it was decided that the new androids had to all watch the same gangster movies. After hours on a do it yourself training manual on the computers, the androids from the freighters learned how to install the graphene partitions and panels, and surprisingly, they were constructing rooms and hallways as shown on their furnished drawings. They had to start on E Deck, so that F Deck was available for offloading from the freighters alongside. The newly trained androids, numbered one through twenty, because there was no other solution, were integrated into the workforce and directed to take orders from Al, Legs and Ace. The graphene partitions were pre-wallpapered with scenic images to give one a feeling of open spaces and trying to match themes of walls ended up with a "Screw it." So the color scheme was like that of an old quilt and surprisingly looked pretty good. It was twenty four seven for everyone but Al, who suffered the criticism when he had to get some sleep. Although he didn't get much sleep, because he had to get the mash room and the still rooms completed and that required a lot of plumbing from scavenged parts.

Over the PA system, Legs was saying, "Meeting in the dining room."

Within minutes twenty eight androids and one human were in what would eventually be the Las Vegas dining room.

Legs said to his companions, "The walls and partitions are almost completed. Boss will explain phase two of the construction. Attention turned to Al and he said, "Boys, we are at a point in the construction that takes some knowledge that none of us have. Now we have to break up into teams that specialize in certain tasks. Hood, back on Earth, sent data disks pertaining to electronics, plumbing and mechanics and in addition, installation instructions for everything to be installed in Las Vegas. You boys are quick learners so you should do well. Me on the other hand am a little slow, but I'm working on the still and mash rooms. In teams of four, you will learn what you can from the data and a team of four will coordinate the work between the teams. Seven, now what in the world do you want?"

"I want to be on the electronics team."

"What in the hell do you know about electronics?"

"I like flashing lights."

Blue said, "I do too."

Al said, "Let me guess. You all like flashing lights."

Legs said, "Boss, go about your business, we'll hash this out."

Teams of four were established with Legs and Ace

directing the work. They decided they would work on one level at a time and finish it and move on. The androids worked remarkably fast and the first level completed was D1 Deck which was entirely of small rooms with inflatable beds. By hotel standards the rooms were nothing to brag about, but were livable, particularly for people who would be drunk. The wiring and what little plumbing there was, was installed first and then the interiors furnished. All of the furnishing had to be constructed of precut graphene panels and glued with epoxy and when a room was completed, it really looked quite nice. On the deck there was a dry shower room and a water recycled sauna. The ship's hull being round complicated the room design, but in all there were thirty rooms on D1 Deck. Then it was on to D2 Deck which was identical. What was the old D Deck now consisted of sixty double bed rooms that were quite small and were no more than sleeping rooms, but the scenic wallpaper helped that situation.

For weeks the twenty eight androids worked nonstop and the end result when finished was the first casino in space. There were twelve levels. The bridge and company offices, the booze level and crew quarters, a huge dining room and kitchen, a large bar and entertainment level, casino game levels, several sleeping room levels, freight levels and storage.

The casino games ran from old school roulette, crap and blackjack to computer slot machines, being simply touch screen monitors and downloaded games on computers.

When the Las Vegas cleared the blackout time, it was for the most part ready for a customer, although there was some fine tuning to be done. The mash room had been in operation for weeks and Al was completely out of water, leaving only a small reserve for drinking.

Little thought was given to the financial end of the project, being how to get credits from the customer and what to do with the credits. It was always assumed to be on a cash basis with credit script. They had come up with a system for the slots, but it was still on a cash basis.

The first email from Hood when the internet was back on line, assured Al that the five thousand gallons of water was on its way and the cost of getting it to him was staggering. The stock was selling like gangbusters and the City Bank of New York wanted to handle all of Las Vegas's finances. *"If you never sell a drink, we have eighty five million credits in the bank."*

Al replied, *"That's your end of it. Send me info how to use other than cash credits; like credit cards and things."*

Hood replied that the bank had programs that Al could download to solve the issue and he said. *"The Captain and I are on our way and we are bringing some friends and they have big bucks they made off the Las Vegas stock. He and the Captain had advertised both on Earth and Mars that you will not be open until two weeks and after we get there. Grand opening of Las Vegas. That's really something."*

"Boss?"

"Yeah?"

Legs said, "Two ships turning towards us."

"Two?"

"What did I say?"

"Ok, ok. It has to be Hood and the Captain and the other ship may be their friends. Call the ships and get a confirmation it's them."

Moments later, "It's them. What do we do? Power up everything in the ship?"

Al replied. "I guess, until we see what the situation is. We'll take them up to the bar first thing. Tell the boys to get in their positions. There must be a bunch of them bringing two ships."

On F2 Deck, being the main entrance to the Las Vegas, Al, Legs and Ace waited for the inner airlock door to open. When it did, Hood, the Captain and about twenty men in suits passed through the contraband detector.

Hood yelled, "We left our heat in the other ship."

Ace replied, "We won't have to plug ya then."

"What about the no shells rule?"

"New rule."

"Oh great. A bunch of gangsters are running this

place?"

Al said, "This is it, just you boys? What about the other ship?"

"We'll talk about that over a Mickey Finn."

There were a lot of introductions between Al and the men in suits while Legs and Ace just edged back and watched.

When all were seated in the bar, androids Blue, Nine, Twelve and Six brought Mickey Finns to the tables and there was twenties orchestra music in the background.

The Captain said to Al, "What I've seen so far is impressive. Did your androids do all of this?"

Legs remarked, "Did *your* androids do all of this?"

The Captain said, "Oops."

Al replied, "Yes."

"I see they are numbered on their hats, and some with colored hats."

"Personnel management. Now about that other ship out there?"

Hood said, "When we received your plans and decided it was a go, we took them to an architectural firm to discuss and explain the project. By the way, they bought stock right off."

Al said, "And?"

They said that although the design was adequate, there were a lot of things required that were missing for a functioning in-space casino complex. I asked the architects if I should contact you and have you incorporate changes into the design, and they said, no. What would be needed could be added at a later date and that you and your androids would not be capable of the installation and would not have the materials. They said it would be better to add them at a later date. At that time the cost would be prohibitive anyway."

Al replied, "I have no idea what you're talking about."

"What I am talking about, is that ship outside and its contents that set us back thirty eight million credits."

"Thirty eight million? What the hell is in it?"

"I'll let Mr. Knisley explain. He will be your guest here for some time. Mr. Knisley?"

"Yes. Al, Legs and Ace. What you have out there is a space ship that is considerably smaller than the Las Vegas. It will be attached to the outside hull of the Las Vegas and with wiring and plumbing be integrated into your systems."

"Ok, what the hell does it do?"

"It totally recycles all of the waste and consumables on board and in fact enhances every system you have onboard and it has a backup nuclear powered generator in the event of power loss. It has an internet connection with your bank to process and manage all of your finances. I could go on, because it has other beneficial qualities."

Hood said, "In reality, the ship has everything we forgot to incorporate or should have. On the onset of the project it would have been a deal breaker. The Captain and I hope we didn't step on your toes too hard and it was terribly expensive."

Ace replied, "We don't have toes, but if we did, you stepped on them hard."

Al said, "Who gives a shit. Ace, do you care how much it costs? How about you, legs?"

After a couple no's, Legs said, "Can I assume there are humans on board that are going to handle all of this?"

The Captain replied, "Yes, the installation people and then some permanent residents. They have their own living quarters, although they might slip over for a drink now and then."

Ace said, "As long as they leave our women alone, *"VIRGINIA SUNRISE."*

One of the men said, "You don't have any women."

Al replied, "I can vouch for that. I'm on a ship with twenty eights unisex androids."

Legs said, "Well, you can run an ad on the internet. Wanted. Good looking woman to live in space thirty million miles from the nearest shopping mall, work her ass off every day, live with twenty eight androids and shack up with a drunk awaiting a murder conviction."

Al said. "Only ninety percent of that is true."

"Well, beg my pardon."

Al asked Hood, "We still have fifty one percent?"

"You're the boss."

"Fine. Let's take the tour. Bring your drinks

gentlemen. We only have a four person elevator, so we will go in groups of four. Anything you want to know, ask an android."

One of the men asked, "Where are the slot machines, I want to try my luck?"

"Go with Blue here. You have cash?"

"Rolling in it, thanks to you boys and I don't mind leaving some of it here."

Ace replied, "We'll do our best, but the slots are on the up and up. If you hit a big win though, talk to Hood and the Captain here, we don't have any cash."

Hood said, "We brought you plenty."

Most of the guests went through all of Las Vegas and eventually ended up in the casino games room or the bar. The Mickey Finns were drank while all of those in the bar talked business pertaining to promoting Las Vegas and getting customers to it. Al more or less just listened to the conversations because Hood and the Captain who were in charge of this aspect of the business. While Al listened, Legs and Ace again watched "*CASINO*" on a table monitor that could also be used for customer gaming. It seems all of the men in the group had connections to businesses or government agencies and how to take advantage of that. In passing, Al heard that it was now illegal for anything like Las Vegas to be placed in space again. This had boosted the Las Vegas stock to astronomical levels. It became apparent that some in the group were responsible for this. It also became apparent that although Las Vegas was a huge business enterprise and Al, Legs and Ace were just a small cog in the wheel, that they were absolutely in control of all aspects of the operation.

At some point the Mickey Finns were showing their effect on the group and Al asked, "How long are you boys going to be staying?"

One replied, "Two weeks."

"Two weeks?"

"We didn't travel sixty million miles to spend the night. You had better get used to that. No one is, except those going between Earth and Mars, on a schedule."

"I suppose we can't expect any more Corp troops?"

The Captain replied, "That's taken care of, R and R, one or two days. What's for dinner?"

"Whatever we have."

Hood said, "We brought a shit pot full of freeze dried stuff and it will be unloaded. For now, anything will do. I'm itching to match wits with an android blackjack dealer."

Al replied, "I would suggest just going with the odds rather than matching wits with Two, the blackjack dealer."

Hood replied, "And they talk, you say?"

"Yeah, but you might have to interpret for your friends. And we are on Eastern standard Earth time. It's now five o'clock in the evening, New York Time."

"I feel at home already. I bet you have that horns and sirens music in your background music library?"

"Of course."

By what was dinner time, everyone was well lubricated and they sat down to an electric candle dinner that android Nine had prepared, drawing from the ten thousand recipes he had in his memory banks and the ingredients he had to work with. Everything considered, it was not that bad.

One of the men said, "A few hours in the casino and we'll try out those inflatable beds."

Hood said to the group, "We'll have another meeting in the morning over Bloody Harrys."

"Was that Bloody Marys?"

"Nope. Bloody Harrys."

A man asked, "Bacon and eggs in the morning?"

Al replied, "If you brought them."

Ace said, "That's an idea. If the customers want to eat what they like, they can bring it."

The Captain said, "Excellent idea, Ace. They bring water and food. That'll save us a shit pot full of money and trouble."

One of the men took out a pen and scribbled this in a notebook.

Hood said, "In the morning then, and good luck out there."

Al asked, "Well gentlemen, what do you think so

far? How were the beds?"

One of the men at breakfast said, "They'll do. I noticed we haven't been charged for the drinks and food and how much are the rooms a night?"

Al replied, "I don't know."

"Well, that could be a problem. Why is that?"

"We have no idea as to the cost of materials and supplies to get them on sight."

Hood said, "That's our fault. Because we have had no steady suppliers or a known delivery method, we just paid what was required to get everything here quick. We have the numbers, but we haven't itemized things. There is no way in hell Al and the boys could know."

Another man said, "I'll note that on the, to do list."

Al asked, "What, to do list?"

The Captain said, "These gentlemen not only have a large investment in the Las Vegas, they are here to get it up and running on the right foot. It will just be a turnkey operation for you by the time they leave."

"It sounds a lot more complicated than I thought."

"Oh, just minor adjustments; you boys did a remarkable job."

Legs said, "An additional space ship and changing everything seems like more than minor adjustments."

Hood said, "Well, you guys are the boss."

Al said, "Go for it. The androids are a little sensitive, but I'm not."

Ace said, "We're not sensitive."

Legs said, "Shut up Ace. Mr. know it all, is ok with it. Let's throw the dog a bone."

Hood said, "Ok, ok, boys, we have company. With your permission, our group here is going to pretend we are a group of two hundred and utilize everything in the Las Vegas. We will individually comment on our experiences and we will all discuss it in a few days. The boys here really want to see the mash room and the still room."

Legs said, "We only have hazmat suits."

One of the men asked, "Hazmat suits? Why do we need a hazmat suit?"

"Oh, nothing lethal. Just don't want you to get your suits dirty. Seeing as how you asked, you can be in the first group. But remember, this is a secret formula."

"I understand."

Al asked, "What about that bunch next door."

The Captain said, "They're ok. They know what to do and they are doing it. Their ship should be attached to the Las Vegas by now."

"How many people over there?"

"Thirty four."

"Thirty four? That's more than we have over here."

"Most will be leaving with us when we leave."

A man in a hazmat suit yelled, "My god, you said it wasn't lethal. What is it?"

Ace replied, "Did you see, *"THE BLOB FROM OUTER SPACE?"*

"No."

"Well, that's it cousin."

"What do you do with that stuff."

"Humans drink it. Did you watch, *"SOYENT GREEN?"*

"What was that about?"

"Eating living things."

"That's alive?"

Ace replied, "So to speak. Right now anyway."

"What's it for."

"Mickey Finns," and the man threw up in his hazmat suit. "Al will explain it all to you. I think we'd better get you out of here."

For two days the group wandered Las Vegas as if in a crowd and had experienced the facilities and took notes.

At another breakfast meeting, a spokesman for the visitors said, "I have accumulated all of the notes and summarized them. It amounts to a list of recommendations. I will start with the theme of the Las Vegas. It appears to be the twentieth century, the fifties through the eighties and a lot of the twenties thrown in. Of course, that is from research because we don't know what Las Vegas casinos and speakeasies looked like then, but we like it and the gangster theme is perfect. Everyone likes being a little naughty when they are out of town. What you do in Vegas, stays in Vegas, kind of thing."

Al replied, "All we had to go on was what was in that era's movies and very little on the internet."

The man said, "Well, the consensus is that we like it, but it needs to be dressed up a little. Starting with the attire of the androids. They look like off the shelf androids."

Ace said, "I object."

Al said, "Shut up, Ace,"

The man continued. "I watched a couple of your early twentieth century gangster movies and we think the old time tailor made suits were great. Nothing stuffy, if you know what I mean. I like the what they call pin stripe and the white shoes. Next, the drinks. Not that Mickey Finns and Bloody Harrys aren't good, but a lot of people don't like orange juice or tomato juice. Some other flavorings are needed."

The meeting continued for a couple hours and was terminated with a plan to make all of the changes. Almost all of the changes could be made with only a few that would have to wait for the next incoming space ship.

"Our next step is for all of the Las Vegas crew to go visit the facilities on the other ship and see anything you want to see."

Hood said, "Well, let's get busy. A portal has been opened between the two ships on F Deck 2.

Al said, "The rest of you make yourself at home. The slot machines and the bar are at your disposal."

Al, Hood, the Captain and twenty eight androids made it to F Deck 2 and entered the newly attached space ship. A man in a hardhat was there to meet them and said, "I'll give you the tour."

Hood said, "Explain to the boys what we have over here."

Smiling, the man in the hardhat said, "Call me Buster. Can I trust a bunch of gangsters?"

Al replied, "No, but I bet you're not squeaky clean yourself."

"No convictions. Anyway, all of your finances will be done over here as well as the logistics for this project. We will have a running inventory and will order as supplies are required. That will be a once a month delivery thing and probably be by the Captain here or Hood. We have the spare nuclear generator that will be wired into your existing wiring. We have the water and waste recycling unit and backup computer systems and we have a system that the Captain will talk to you about later. The dry laundry and ultra violet sterilization will be done over here as well, by one of my crew. The object of this ship is so that you boys from the Las Vegas will have nothing to do but operate the Las Vegas and of course make the booze."

"Right now, I have people ready to dye reams of cloth for your new outfits and sew them up for you. Just waiting for the theme."

Hood said, "Early mobster."

"Cagney stuff?"

Ace said, "You know, Cagney?"

"I know of him. Flicker network."

Al said, "We've seen enough. It's in good hands."

"Well, thanks, Boss."

CHAPTER SIX

FLIGHT OR FIGHT

Back on the Las Vegas, Al said to the group, "Ace and I are going to be running a batch through the still. You are welcome to help if you like."

One man said, "Not me," and the others agreed with that.

Hood replied, "With some of your boys, we'll get the last of the freight off the Captain's ship."

"Sounds good. By the way, I want to show you something, Hood. Follow me."

Away from everyone, Al said, "Ok, what's the skinny on that whatever it is system you were supposed

176

to tell me about"

Hood whispered, "A laser cannon."

"A laser cannon? What in the hell am I supposed to do with a laser cannon?"

"Protection."

"From what, a pirate ship?"

"Yes. At two miles it will punch a small hole in anything. Not enough to depressurize a ship instantly, but enough to get their attention and they won't want any more holes."

"The Captain and I are in charge of all traffic to the Las Vegas and it is by reservation only. Any ship that we clear will have a code sign and any that doesn't have the code sign could be trouble. There is still no law out here. If you control it, you own it."

"What about some of your reservation people when inside the Las Vegas?"

"On F Deck 2, there is a box labeled CC for crowd control. A lot of hand held devices to discourage such an event or for that part a belligerent customer."

Al replied, "This will be a New York City bar. All of the customers are belligerent."

Hood said, "Use your own discretion."

"Hell, one of these androids can pick a guy up and throw him against a wall with one arm."

"You're the casino boss. Whatever it takes. If you have to bust some heads, go for it. This damned place had better make a profit or we can use those stock certificates for ass wipe."

Smiling, Al said, "I've never owned a casino that went broke."

"Oh, that's reassuring. No one in two hundred years has owned a casino. I'll help with the still. I need to get my hands dirty."

Al replied, "I've found that a little after-shave in the hazmat suit helps."

Hood said to Al, Legs and Ace, "I'm sorry that we put a kink in your plans, but if you are going to open a casino in space, it might as well be a good one. It had better work out or we are in deep shit. Among other things, we have discovered that two weeks is way too long for a stay. We're going to go with one week for the customers. We already have a backlog of reservations for at least six hundred. The first load of two hundred has already left and will be here in three weeks, along with everything we ordered."

Al asked, "Is everything on schedule next door?"

"Leaving a crew of eight. Two craft workers and six nerds. One of the craft workers is making those outfits for you and your boys."

Legs said, "I guess Ace and I will have be communicating with the nerds."

"Ok. My friends are waiting for me downstairs. You might practice with that thirty eight pea shooter I brought you and all of the glassware that Legs and Ace break you can replace with that 3D printer. See you boys down the road."

On the bridge, Al asked Legs and Ace, "What are we going to do with these twenty six androids for six weeks?"

Legs said, "We set up the internet movies on the slot machine monitors to play around the clock. All of the casino and gangster movies. We should check the boys next week though and see how they're doing."

Ace said, "I want to be a pit boss. If there is any cheating goin on, I'll know it."

Legs replied, "Hey, that's my job."

"Said who?"

"Boys. You can both be pit bosses. I don't trust you waiting tables and serving drinks. Do what you're best at, standing and watching someone else work."

Ace replied, "Isn't it your bedtime with a drink? You've been up three hours."

Legs asked Al, "What's your job going to be?"

"Management and casino greeter."

"The only thing you can manage is getting a drink to your mouth."

Ace said, "He should work the bar, he's a natural."

Al replied, "My thought exactly. Hood said a couple of our female customers are going to do some entertaining on stage in the bar."

"What kind of entertaining?"

Legs replied. "They're humans. Nothing would surprise me."

Al asked, "Do all of the androids know their jobs?"

"Well, certainly they know their jobs. We are going to have a rehearsal a day before the guests arrive. You being management and all, you can see what you should have done."

"Lighten up, Legs. I'll want you to do your act on stage in the bar."

"What act?"

"Acting like you know something. Are the outfits ready?"

Legs answered, "I don't know, ask the manager."

Al replied, "Seriously."

"Next week."

"What outfit did you ask for?"

"George Raft's suit, hat and shoes"

"Ace, how about you?"

"Cagney. How about you, Boss?"

"Humphrey Bogart. He always gets the women."

"Well, this should be something to see. Even a blind chicken fins a kernel of corn now and then."

Al replied, "There are women coming on board you know. I'll give it a shot. Even a kernel now and then is better than no kernels at all."

Legs said, "You'll probably end up *getting* shot. That reminds me. I guess it's the greeter's job to get them all through the contraband detector."

"Why, of course it is. Have you two familiarized yourself with those stun guns Hood brought?"

"Yes, and you know what that means?"

"What?"

"Our shoes have to be made with rubber soles."

"That's not all bad. It sounds like a herd of shod horses tromping around here now."

The ship that was now referred to as the Fun Flight would be in in two days and the three were dressed like they stepped out of a gangster movie.

Ace said, "I hate to say it Boss, but you look like the real thing. Your packin heat aren't you?"

"It's not loaded. Just for effect."

"You?"

"Ankle holster."

"Good touch."

Legs said, "Ok, let's do the rehearsal. Right from the top. The androids are in place and the place is powered up."

The rehearsal went without a hitch other than Al missed a couple of his lines. And of course, an android never misses a line.

On the bridge, Ace said, "Piece of cake. Three is working the cage so that will be busy right off and I'll help out. We have chips, one credit through a hundred credits. The Hideout ship next door is online. I ran a couple transactions through, no problem."

"Hideout?"

"Yeah, me and Legs named it."

Al said, "I'm a little nervous."

Legs replied, "Well, if we had a nerve, we would

probably know what the hell you are talking about."

Al replied, "Wondering if everything is going to go ok."

"That's nervous?"

"Yeah."

"Me, too."

Ace said, "The ship will dock in two hours."

Al replied, "Well, let's get everything fired up and get our smiley faces on."

"Androids don't have smiley faces."

"That's just one more thing they don't have."

Legs asked, "Are these two hundred going to be like you?"

"I have a hunch they aren't. You have to be rich and special to afford a trip out here."

Ace asked, "How much shit are we supposed to take off of these people?"

"Well, I'm not taking any. Those that are a problem, we'll just kick off the ship. I'm headed for the entrance; you boys are on your own. The bar will only hold a hundred, so I'll send you boys up a hundred to the gaming room. They can order drinks up there."

Al could hear the people through the airlock door and when it opened the people started walking through the contraband detector carrying bottles of water and forming a crowd behind Al. Two were stopped and showed metal implant slips and when all two hundred were in, Al got their attention and loudly explained the rules and divided the crowd into two groups. The first group he took to the bar and the second he directed to the gaming room. All decided to take the stairs rather than wait on the elevator rides. Al hadn't realized how quiet it had been in the ship for months, but he did now. Nearly a hundred drinks were already on the tables in the bar and two androids and Al gathered the water in carts. As the crowd drank their Mickey Finns and ordered more from the androids, Al went from table to table assigning one room per two people and explained that if the two did not sleep together, they could stagger their sleeping periods.

Six hours passed and the sounds of the background music and slot machine themes filled the gaming room and could be heard down into the bar level. People were asking about dinner and directions to the bar and their rooms. Twenty eight androids were running their hind ends off keeping up with things.

In the bar, a guy stood up at his table and said, "Hey droid, where's my damned drink." The guy then said "Those dumb ass androids never were worth a damn."

Android Fifteen said to him, "You are going to have to sit down and shut up."

"No damned android is going to tell me what to do."

Fifteen raised his Taser and shot the guy in the chest and he collapsed on the table with his friends looking wide eyed.

"Take him to his room. Now."

The guy's buddies gathered him up and left the bar with his heels dragging on the floor."

The android said to the customers, "Any other orders while I'm here."

About the same thing happened upstairs in the gaming room, but Legs grabbed the guy by the shirt and lifted him off the ground with one hand and threw him into the hallway.

A few more of these type confrontations and word around the Las Vegas was that you didn't want to mess with this gang. Knowing there was no law in neutral space, the crowd had edged towards being out of control until they realized what they were up against. The gangster outfits the androids were wearing represented who they really were, not a bunch of mechanical devices to be manipulated.

Al constantly circulated among the customers with the only smile they were going to see from the crew and answered questions as he sweet talked them. The appearance was that Al was definitely the Boss and had control over all of the good or bad things the androids did. If an android roughed you up, it was assumed it was on the Boss's orders.

For the customers, the first day was wild, the second day apprehensive and by the third day they were also adopting some gangland attitudes and Al was the Boss. They felt like they were part of the gang and wined and dined, gambled, sang and carried on little different than people in the speakeasies over two hundred years earlier. "What they did in Vegas, stayed in Vegas."

And yes, there were women who got up on stage and entertained and with a big screen monitor showing nineteen twenties flapper girls doing the Charleston on tables, many of the women in the bar did the same. It was a twenty four- seven, wild time for seven days and when the Fun Flight left, all of the customers were in the best of moods and thanked Al and the androids for the good time had by all.

Just like that it was over and the Las Vegas was again quiet as a tomb.

Al said to Ace and Legs, "I'm going to sleep for two days?"

Ace asked, "Who's going to clean up this mess?"

"I thought you boys could handle it."

"It's all for one and one for all, not just all for one."

Al said, "What in the hell does that mean?"

Legs replied, "You don't work, nobody works."

"Why don't you just say that?"

"I just did."

"Ok, ok. R and R for everybody. You androids had better catch up on your movies. Maybe there is one out there you haven't seen."

Ace replied, "I bet you even dream about getting shitfaced."

"Did I get drunk anytime this week?"

"No. Totally out of character. You are to be

commended."

Al said, "I wonder how we did in the cage?"

Legs replied, "We would have done a lot better if that drunk idiot hadn't hit that jackpot."

"They'll hear about that on Earth and they'll be banging on our door to get in."

"That's what I'm worried about."

This was a good opportunity for the men in the Hideout next door to visit and they were welcome anytime. The liquor was free, but for the gaming, they were on their own. They frequently visited the small theater and watched movies with the androids.

In two weeks another group of two hundred arrived along with a lot of provisions. It went about the same as the previous bunch, but their old friend's, One, Two and Three were with them. While in the bar, they waved Al to their table and One said, "I'm impressed. How did you do on that last bunch?"

Al replied, "I don't know. Accounting takes care of that."

"You don't know? Well, if it had been bad you would know. You have a swinging deal here and no other gang has a casino out here. We know. We leaned on some people real hard and still couldn't muscle in."

Two said, "And to make it worse, you blackballed us on any piece of the action. We don't take too kindly to that."

Al replied, "You should have bought stock."

"We don't buy stock. We don't buy anything."

One said, "It's not too late to do the right thing."

"What's the right thing?"

"A piece of your interest and we can help you run the place. We have some good ideas."

Al got up and said, "You boys have a good time, drinks are on me."

The week ended and the fun flight ship left with another bunch of happy customers, except for three gangsters on the flight.

Al said to Legs and Ace, "I'm looking for trouble from those three. I don't know how, but we'll see. The next flight here is from Mars, so I don't think there will be a problem, but the first one from Earth, we had better look long and hard at the people getting off the Fun Flight."

Legs said, "We have time to think about a defense. They are more apt to disable our ship than start something in the casino. Our boys can handle any rough stuff in here and they know it."

Ace said, "We had better have Hood screen everyone coming on the next Earth trip."

"Yep. I can't hardly stand the looks of this mess for two days, but it beats the hell out of cleaning it up. I need a rest anyway. I have to start up a new batch of mash. How are we doing on water the customers are bringing."

"We're ahead of the game."

"Good. They left a lot of food, too."

Al said, "Did you ever go camping?"

"What in the hell is camping?"

"That's when you take twice as much food as you need out into the mountains."

"Never had the occasion."

"I suppose not. It's not all it's cracked up to be anyway."

"Cracked up to be?"

The Mars flight arrived and was full of Corp troops and Al said, "We're going to have trouble with this bunch. They are going to start off with a binge drunk and they don't have much money to lose playing the slots."

Ace said, "We'll help you out in the bar."

"Good, I'll need some muscle. Now please, don't kill one of them. It's not good for business. I'll herd them up to the bar and the gaming room. They already have their room numbers. When they start passing out, we'll just put them to bed. I hope they are all friends because they are going to be waking up with someone in the bed with them."

Al was right and after two hours of drinking, some of them were getting a little brave. Having heard about the discipline on the Las Vegas, every one of them thought he could whip an android. Well, android's reflexes are not human and a thrown punch was a waste of effort, but the repercussion was certain. Picked up and dropped or thrown across the room was enough to settle the argument. After six hours, Al said to Legs, "Well, your boys have managed to beat up half the troops."

"Any fatalities?"

"Not that I know of."

"I told the boys to handle them with kid gloves."

On the bridge and in contact with Hood on Earth, Hood assured Al that he did the best he could on background checks of the people on the next flight. He was at least certain none of the people were gang members from New York City."

Al replied, *"Well, maybe we'll get lucky and the boys just forgot about it."*

Hood replied, *"They don't forget. A pride thing you know."*

Ace said, "A ship left the traffic lane and cloaked."

Al sent to Hood, *"Well, we are going to have company. I have to get off."*

"You have the laser cannon."

"Yes we do, we'll see."

"How long, ace?"

"Five hours."

"Legs, what do you think they're going to do?"

"My guess is that they will try to cut the main power supply on both of our ships and dock with the Hideout next door. The Hideout has control of all of our electrical functions over here."

"What does that mean?"

"They can black us out over here, go to zero gravity and other things that would raise hell with us. During this, they would gain entrance to the Las Vegas with weapons and take us out."

Al said, "Well, that's bullshit. They aren't moving in on our territory. Do we know how to use that damned laser cannon?"

"Yes. The crafts people mounted it and they have been practicing with it. We don't know shit about it. It will have to be operated from over there."

"Ace, you stay here, me and Legs are going next door. Let them know we're coming."

"Right, Boss."

"Buster, you know we have company coming?"

"Those ass holes you told me about?"

Almost certain, but we had better be right. Is the laser cannon fired up?"

"Ready to roll. That ship will be busy patching a hole for some time."

Al asked, "Can you make the beam larger?"

"No. That's a built in safety factor in case of an accident. But we can make a lot of little holes."

"If that's our boys, I want that ship to look like a loaf of Swiss cheese. No more mister nice guys."

"Fine, but we have to see them before we can shoot them."

Al asked, "They have to uncloak don't they, to do

anything to us?"

"Yes."

"Well, the second it comes uncloaked, eat it up."

Buster replied, "It'll take a little bit to target them and we sure as hell don't want to hit their nuclear reactor."

"Whatever it takes, but be quick. I'm thinking they will want to negotiate a deal and that will take a minute or two and we'll know then we are getting the right bunch."

"You'll have to be here for all of this. You flick your fingers and it's a go for the laser. Do you think those big shots will be on board?"

"Oh, hell no. They'll have some of their boys do the dirty work. We'll work on that problem later. Nothing like a little gang war to make things interesting."

Buster said, "Well, I don't want my people hurt, they are just working stiffs."

"Well, let's just ice this bunch then."

Buster asked, "What do you think, Legs?"

"Go for it."

Al, Legs and Buster watched over the shoulder of one of the technicians on the Hideout.

Legs said, "It should be anytime now. We're patched into the bridge of the Las Vegas so if they say anything we'll be able to hear it. They will probably be off our port in line with all of the junction boxes between the Las Vegas and the Hideout. We don't know if they are going to come to the ships in suits or use something like lasers."

The speaker on the main computer said, "Al, your number friends have an offer you can't refuse."

The technician said, "I have them off the port, and on the monitor appeared a modest size space ship.

Buster targeted the ship and Al flicked his fingers.

The laser beam couldn't be seen in the vacuum of space, but a small black dot appeared on the hull of the ship, and then another and another until there were hundreds and a fog of atmosphere was coming from all of them.   There didn't seem to be any effect on the ship, but the escaping atmosphere from within acted like small jets and the ship began to spin and drift away into space.

Buster said, "It's a done deal. They probably got a call off. I'm sure we're going to hear about this."

Al replied. "It'll be a while. In the meantime, we have a fun flight coming in three days."

Back on the Las Vegas, Al, Legs and Ace sat in the bar and discussed what had just happened and Al asked the two, "Did it bother you boys rubbing out that bunch?"

Ace replied, "You live by the sword, you die by the sword."

Al said, "On that note, let's watch *"WHITE HEAT,"* we haven't seen it in weeks."

"*You* haven't seen it in weeks?   That's the boy's

downstairs favorite. They like the part where the human goes up in smoke."

"Do I have to remind them about the scrap yard?"

"Speaking of that, some of the boys are malfunctioning. They need some new components and batteries."

"We didn't buy those damned androids all that long ago."

"They weren't new when we bought them, Sheriff."

"And what's that going to cost?"

"A lot."

"What's a lot?"

"How in the hell would I know. It's not like going to the store and buying a loaf of bread. We'll have to have Hood make the arrangements."

Al asked, "So what does all of this mean?"

Legs replied, "It means that they will be dropping out one at a time over the next three months."

"Would it be cheaper to just replace them?"

"I don't know. Go down and tell the boys they are going to be replaced if the parts are too expensive."

"Sorry. Ok, get ahold of Hood and tell him what we need and we need it pronto. Let's watch that damned movie."

The three sat in the small dark theater watching "*WHITE HEAT*," starring James Cagney as Jack Cody, a maniacal mobster. Jack Cody is on top of one of many large fuel tanks and the coppers are shooting at him. He is hit several times and finally shoots into the fuel tank below him that ignites in flame. With the flames engulfing him, he yells, "I made it, Ma. Top of the world," and the tank below him explodes.

With the lights coming on, Ace said, "Now that's what I call a movie."

Legs said, "Probably twenty five years old and filthy rich and could never get enough. Had to make it to the top. Well, he did."

Al said, "He probably owned a casino."

"Probably. The boys next door said we aren't doing all that good. Those Corp troops aren't worth messing with."

"Hood had better get us more fun flights up here. He should be calling about the android parts."

"He had better, we have a one armed bartender."

"Al, Legs and Ace

"Scuttlebutt around town. A ship was lost between here and Mars. Owners aren't saying a thing and didn't report it. I'm not even going to ask.

I rounded up the parts in a manner of speaking. All parts for RTR model androids are used parts. The parts are ridiculously priced. It was a lot cheaper to just buy the whole android than a few parts. The Captain and I will be bringing twenty androids for parts. Some work and some don't work very well, but still functioning. Tell Legs and Ace, good enough to fly a space ship or do laundry.

To more important matters. The income off of Las Vegas isn't what it was supposed to be. We have been cooking the books to keep the stock prices up. Right now we have millions in the bank from stock sales, so we can do this for some time. Anything you can do to increase the revenue, do it. The Captain said to fire up the 3D printer and make fancy bottles. We have some new flavorings we're bringing. We're having to grease the palms of a lot of people down here. There was talk about eliminating the neutral zone, but we put a kibosh on that.

If a ship shows up with call numbers 999, sell him all of the booze you can. We have already settled on a price. The Captain, we will call 999 is Mexican, so have one of the boys learn Spanish.

Hood."

Al said to Legs and Ace, "Twenty more damned androids; they're running out of our ears now."

Ace said, "Running out our ears?"

"Too many."

Legs replied, "Well, one human is too many."

"For parts, and most of them don't work. Lovely, we have a veteran's hospital here."

"Well, I'm sure none of them are hiding from a hangman's noose."

"If I had a hangman's noose, I would use it."

Legs said, "Ace, where's that one you made."

Al said, "Seriously guys, what are we going to do

with them?"

Legs said, "They can stay with you in the broom closet."

"Ok, ok. What about making more money? A week here and a week there isn't cutting it."

Legs replied, "Hood and the Captain are going to have to open this place up to ships besides their fun flights. I know there are ships that would stop; we hear the chatter on their transmissions. With the extra androids, we can handle it."

"If any of them work."

"They can all do something."

"Ok, we'll run it by Hood and the Captain when they get here. For now, the prices in Las Vegas on everything just went up."

The Fun Flight arrived and it was the same old thing. Of course there were the few that had to test the androids and that didn't work out well for them. Their week was spent in their rooms healing up. There was no indication anyone knew of a missing ship and it was assumed that this was just an issue between Al and the New York mob. The prices of everything went up except on the games. The blackjack tables and slots would have the same revenues, but the increase in price on the drinks and food would help considerably. Of course there were some moments when a customer would yell, "Jackpot," and Al would just cringe. Like Legs and Ace, he hadn't given a damn about any money he made off the casino, because there was no place to spend it. But now it wasn't money for him, it was money to keep the Las Vegas going. Although Al, Legs and Ace complained about the work, they were into it now. They were big shot gangsters and liked it. It was like one big gangster movie and they had leading roles.

There were more fun flights and finally Hood and the Captain showed up with the twenty androids and they were a rough looking bunch. No suits and caps and by human standards they were naked. A couple with an arm hanging limp and some dragging a leg.

Al said, "Ace, herd them into that room on F Deck 2. We'll be in the bar," and he, Legs, Hood and the Captain took the elevator up."

In the bar, Hood said, "We have about every artificial flavor under the sun with us. Did you get the bottles made?"

Android Eight is working on them upstairs."

The captain said, "Tell me about the mob's missing ship."

Al told the story and the Captain said, "You know you haven't seen the last of that bunch."

"I suppose. It could get real nasty up here. I want to train a couple of the androids to replace the crew on the ship next door. Those people don't have a dog in this fight. We need to get them out of here."

Hood asked, "Do you want to make a deal with the

New York bunch?"

"No."

"Do you want to just close up shop? We can dump our stock and still be millionaires."

Al said, "And then what? I can't go anywhere and spend the money and androids can't own anything. Me, Legs and Ace would just as soon ride it out. We aren't the first people that others tried to muscle out. We'll see how it goes."

"Ok, it's up to you three."

Al explained to Hood and the Captain that if they wanted the Las Vegas to be a success, they would have to have more flights in.

Hood said, "You're throwing caution to the wind anyway, so we'll open it up to anyone that can get there. We have the three month blackout period coming up, so we'll put the word out during that time. You'll have a load of freight coming in before then. I'll have another laser cannon on board."

A few fun flights later and the freight ship arrived, the Las Vegas entered the blackout period and repairs were made to the androids. They all worked to some degree and were assigned jobs they could do when they opened back up. Expecting more business, gaming area was added to the attached Hideout space ship and a bar as well. Additional sleeping rooms were added and a small snack bar. A large alcohol supply was stored and some bottled in fancy bottles at twice the normal price.

The three months passed and two ships showed up without any notice and two hundred and fifty customers were dispersed with all going through the contraband detector. It was apparent that they were all wealthy and they had to be or they wouldn't be there.

Legs said to Al, "They might be rich folk, but some of them look real shady."

"That's because they are real shady. All of our boys have Tasers?"

"Yeah."

"Well, we just have to handle the situation."

There were more fights, a few heads bumped by the androids and a couple Taser events and listening to "Do you know who I am?" But after a few days it settled down and on day seven they were gone.

It was no time until another ship showed up with two hundred on board and it was the same thing all over again. The good news was that the Las Vegas was taking in a vast amount of money. Word must have spread on Earth and Mars, because they all brought water and in fact the water containers were becoming a problem. Hundreds were ejected into space because they were underfoot everywhere.

Hood and the Captain arrived with some shareholders between customer flights and Hood told Al, Legs and Ace that they wanted to have a shareholders meeting in the bar.

Twenty humans, Legs and Ace sat at tables and

Hood said to Al, Legs and Ace, "Well boys, we have big problems."

Al asked, "How big?"

"Couldn't be worse. The gangs in New York, Chicago and Los Angeles are pissed and they are going to make a move on us. We are siphoning off all of their high roller customers. They have big money poker, blackjack, roulette and the like, but they have to stay small because it's against the law. Their high rollers can come up here and let it all hang out. They are tired of that sneaking in the back door bullshit."

"Well, the New York gang tried it before."

"This is different. Through a snitch, we are led to believe that the mobs on Earth are pooling their money and are fitting a ship to come up here."

Al said, "And? They uncloak and we Swiss cheese it."

"I wish. The new ship, at great expense to them, is covered with a reflective surface."

Legs said, "Our laser cannons are useless."

The Captain said, "That's right."

Al said, "So we are just supposed give them the Las Vegas?"

"Yes, or they are going to destroy it with laser cannons and all of you with it."

"Well, that's the shits. But they can go to hell. What are our options? Can we just cloak and move somewhere else?"

The Captain said, "This ship can only cloak for eight

hours and not again for sixteen. The reactor can't handle it."

Legs asked, "When is this all going to happen?"

"We just have to go off what the snitch told us and that is about three weeks from now."

Al said, "We're all dead whether it is the mobs or the authorities. The androids will be scrap and I'll be hanging."

Hood said, "There isn't a damned thing we can do for you out here. We are going to have a financial nightmare at home no matter what happens."

Al said, "If there isn't anything we can do, you boys might as well enjoy yourselves. Me, Legs and Ace have some talking to do. Everything's on the house. Just ask for credit slips at the cage for the games."

On the bridge, Al, Legs and Ace sat and Al said, "Alright you two, come up with something."

Legs said, "Come up with something? How about you, you're the mastermind."

Al replied, "They have got us. We can cloak for eight hours and then in another eight hours when they catch us, it's lights out."

Ace said, "Can we ram them?"

"You want to think about that. What the hell good would that do?"

"Just a thought."

"Well, don't have another one."

"Ok, I won't. What are we going to do? What's your thought?"

"My thought? Well, let's see. I started with only what I was wearing, worked my way up to part owner of the largest casino in the universe, have untold millions of credits, busted some heads and killed a few hoodlums. But unlike Cagney, I'm not going to burn, yelling, "Ma, I made it. Top of the world, Ma.""

Ace said, "We're right back to my question, what are we going to do?"

Legs answered, "We run for it cloaked."

Al said, "With an eight hour jump on them, they'll never catch us if we keep moving."

Ace asked, "Where are we going?"

Al replied, "How in the hell would I know? What I do know though, is that I am on a spaceship heading into outer space with forty eight androids and a hundred and fifty gangster movies. That ought to be a fun trip."

"You forgot about the five hundred gallons of alcohol on board."

"There had to be one bright spot in this nightmare."

Legs said, "The broom closet thing still applies."

"That would be cruel and unusual punishment."

"Better you than us. We have a couple weeks, so lighten up."

Al said, "I'm going to bed and have a nightmare and see if I can top this one."

"Need a wakeup call?"

"For what?"

For two days Al sulked in his room and on the third

day he joined Legs and Ace in the casino theater. "What are we watching boys?"

"*THE INVISIBLE MAN*," replied Ace.

"I haven't seen that one."

"You'd like it. It would give you some hope."

"Al said, "Let's go in the bar and talk.""

"All of the androids are in there; we ran them out of the theater."

"Well, run them back in. I need a drink."

In the bar, Al said to his partners, "I have been doing some thinking. I have come up with a hodgepodge of thoughts and I need you guys to fill in the blanks."

Ace said, "I don't have a clue about hodgepodges of thoughts."

"A collection of thoughts."

Legs said, "More than one and somehow they go together?"

"Yes, sort of. Here is what I have been thinking. We don't want to be terminated and we don't want to take a never ending trip into space. The people that would terminate us are the governments of Mars and Earth and the Earth mobs. What do you think?"

"What do you mean, what do we think? We already know this."

"What would prevent us being terminated?"

Ace replied, "The governments and the mobs deciding not to do it."

"Exactly, That's our problem. What do we do to

make them decide not to? The mob will kill us on sight and it's perfectly legal and that is the same for the governments."

Legs said, "Can we get to something we don't know?"

Al said, "I'm going to float an idea by you two and I want you to think on it."

"What in the hell does float an idea mean?"

"Up for discussion."

"Ok. Float it."

"We travel towards Mars and get just inside the non-neutral space. In Mars jurisdiction and we park."

"That's it?"

"That's it. That's what I want you boys to work on and come up with a solution that would make this possible and advantageous for us."

Legs said, "I can see some pros and cons."

"Not now. Tomorrow. Think on it."

"You're serious?"

"Yep."

Back in the bar the next day, Al said. "Well boys, what do you have for me?"

Legs replied, "You hand us your mess and then say, fix it. There is no fixing this."

"Aw come on. Where is that android ingenuity? Let's just kick it around a bit."

Legs said, "Ace, did you hear that? Kick it around."

"I heard."

Al said, "Let's assume it's a lost cause and just discuss hair brained ideas. Ok, we get into Mars jurisdiction and then what?"

Legs replied, "They come out and arrest you and no telling what they do to us."

"But, the gangsters can't rub us out because they would be breaking the law and would definitely get caught. And, the Mars authorities won't terminate us because of their laws. So at least we are still alive."

"You are, but there is no law against putting androids in the trash compactor."

Al replied, "Understood. So how do we deal with Mars so they won't arrest me and snuff you two? Seriously. I'm going to mix a drink while you boys talk it over."

Back at the table after slowly mixing a drink, Al asked, "What do you think?"

Legs said, "We make a proposal to the Mars and Earth governments."

"What kind of proposal? Before you go any further. Can we get back into the neutral space before they get to us?"

"Yes, if we stay on top of things."

"Good. Go ahead."

Legs replied, "Rather hastily, Ace and I have made a list of things favorable to the Mars government and a list of unfavorable. We tell them that Mars has a society and social laws whereby no one wants to live there permanently. Their government is too damn conservative and rigid and everyone lives underground. There is no gambling or social drinking allowed. Almost everyone there goes to Earth on leave or vacation at great expense to Mars. We can park the Las Vegas in orbit around Mars and abide by all of the laws of Mars, not directly pertaining to a casino. We pay heavy taxes on casino profits to the government. Alphonse Bruni to be pardoned by Mars and Earth and the androids on the Las Vegas, given the honorary status of Mars citizenship. The Las Vegas will be manned entirely by androids. This project will be of benefit to the Mars economy."

Al said, "What about me?"

"The mob boss never works at the casino, he just visits."

"Well that's all very interesting, but why will they buy this bill of goods?"

"Bill of goods?"

"This bullshit."

Legs replied, "We have to offer another proposal."

"What would that be?"

"We park the Las Vegas just inside the neutral space and let the Earth mobs run it. All of the liquor and drugs you want to take home with you. And of course an online casino for those that want to gamble at home. Not to mention the ladies of the evening available and the porno material for sale. Being that close, the government could never control a ten hour trip out to the Las Vegas by Mars people."

Al said, "They are never going to buy this."

"Probably not, killer. But we can run it by them. We had some of those Mars judges and politicians up here and they had smiles on their faces."

"What have we got to lose? We still have the run like hell option. Let's write it up real formal like and get it off to Mars. If we don't hear back by the time we see the gangs coming for us, well take off cloaked to nowhere. Mars will hash this around for no telling how long if it's a possibility or we will get it right back rejected."

Two days later the proposal was sent to Mars and this was after a lot of fine tuning was done to it.

Al said, "Well, this is going to take a while. Probably months, we don't have. We'll just ride it out. We've been neglecting the movies and the Mickey Finns, let's watch something weird."

Ace answered, "Like what?"

"I don't know. How about the best foreign film. In computer lingo. Best foreign film of nineteen seventy five. How about that?"

"What was the best foreign film of nineteen seventy five?"

"Hell, I don't know. Have you seen those candy machines that had a *take a chance*?"

"Never encountered one. What would I be doing at

a candy machine?"

"Forget it. I'll search Google for a movie."

"There it is, best foreign film of nineteen seventy five. *"TAI NI POI."*

Ace said "What in the hell does that mean?"

"I don't know. Have you seen it before?"

"No."

"Well, that's surprising."

Five minutes into the movie, when two Orientals wearing cowboy hats were riding a fire breathing dragon, large text came up on the screen. *"The Government of Mars accepts your proposal. A message will be coming within the hour."*

Al yelled, "You're shitting me."

Legs said, "Ace, did you put that on there?"

"Wasn't me."

Al said, "That's impossible. Are they nuts?"

Ace said, "What's nuts."

"Shut up, Ace. Let's get upstairs. Maybe this movie monitor screwed up, like it left out the *don't.*"

Al ran up the flights of stairs and sat in front of his monitor and it read, *"The Government of Mars accepts your proposal. A message will be coming within the hour."*

Not designed for running up stairs, Legs and Ace entered and looked over Al's shoulder and Ace said,

"That's what it says."

The three sat watching their monitors and within the hour a message flashed, "*Call me at 22-287-8767. The President of Mars.*"

Al asked, "How in the hell am I going to call him on the phone?"

Ace replied, "I'll show you."

"I can make a phone call from here?"

"Yes."

"Well, kiss my ass. You mean I have been going through this email shit for a couple years and I could have made a phone call?"

Ace replied, "If you had asked."

"Get him on the damned phone."

"Well, you don't have to get huffy."

Al replied, "Huffy? If that means I am about ready to ring your neck, yes, I'm getting huffy."

"*Hello.*"

"*Mr. President?*"

"*Yes. Bruni?*"

"*Yes, Sir.*"

"*Well, Mr. Bruni. The powers that be on Mars have decided to take you up on your offer. We have had some good reports on you and your business enterprise. To be brief, we are experiencing some trouble here with the kind of services you furnish and we want none of it on Mars. Some input from influential people here and the Corp on your operation was quite influential. There are a few minor issues in your proposal that need to be clarified, but can be worked out quickly.*

Al said hesitantly, "*How about the murder charge?*"

"*Oh, that charge was dropped weeks after you left here for Earth. That was to be taken care of when you arrived there.*"

"*Dropped?*"

"*Yes. It was your associate's wife that killed him. Something about a motorcycle he bought. She was convicted of murder and selling drugs.*"

"*You have to be shitting me. Mars and Earth have been after me for two years.*"

"*Yes, for stealing a spaceship. That has legally been ironed out.*"

Gritting his teeth, Al said, "*We are looking forward to our business arrangement, Sir. But, one thing. There is a spaceship full of goons heading for us and they intend to blow this ship all to hell.*"

The President replied, "*I know. Get your ship inside our jurisdiction and there will be two Corp gunships there to see this doesn't happen. One other item. It seems that your facility is a little on the small side for our purposes. What do you think about doubling it in size? Just think on it. It will be on our dime.*"

"*Well, Sir, I'm momentarily over being pissed off. Top of the world, Ma.*"

The President asked, "*You like Cagney?*"

THE END

ABOUT THE AUTHOR

BOOKS BY TOM NORTON

"Waterfall"
"The Dark Side Rocket"
"A Montana Gold Miner"
"Columbia Basin Hunting and Fishing
Beginning 1943"
"A Slice of Time in Rural America (1917)"
"Hot Rain"
"Irish Gold"
"Who's Right? Who's Wrong?"
"Martin-Martin the Whale Hunter"
"Grays, Why They Are Here"
"The Alien Gold Plate"
"A Simple Programming Error"
"Slave Gold"
"Balloonatics"
"Attu DC-3 Lost"
"Ice and Spears"
"Feliz's Missiles"
"Tenoch's Aztec Gold"
"On Pa's Farm 1910-1917"
"Buffalo Ponees"
"The McMillan Saga 1862"
"Story of the Century"
"1850"
"America's Women and Children"
"Yukon Gold"
"Vasero Bounty Hunters 1836"

"The Forbidden King of Dristavia"
"Piss Ant"
"Cannibal Gold"
"2050 It Isn't Pretty"
"Hanford's First Kids"
"Macumba" Slave Ship Captain
"Captain and Macumba"
"Hard Times 1867"
"Trump, Grandpa, Grandma, Susie & Jimmie"
"Tom Norton's Book Directory"
"Juan & Achak 1868"
"Outer Space Casino"
"Penal Colony"
"Dust Bowl Okies"
"A Piece of the Action"
"Kill Uncle Fred"
"The Roberts Boys   On The Run"
"Cane & Pone Unlikely gun fighters"
"Earth Three   Princes and Demons"
"Karl's War Mob & Nazis"
"Sequoyah's Tears"
"50,000 BC And Me"
"This is Nonsense George's Ark"
"Hoist All Sails"
"Intruder and TRN---Buffalo Soldiers"
"Proxima Centauri"
"Meeli and Captain"
"Rebels Yankees and the Kimbles"
"Planet M27"
"The Madam And The Gold Miner"
"Molly's Texas Oil"
"A Deserter Hero"

Made in United States
North Haven, CT
16 September 2023

41626558R00136